THE MENSTRUAL COUPÉ

THE MENSTRUAL COUPÉ

Stories

SHAHINA K. RAFIQ

Translated by

PRIYA K. NAIR

First published in Malayalam in 2016 by Mathrubhumi
This translation first published in India in 2024 by Hachette India
(Registered name: Hachette Book Publishing India Pvt. Ltd)
An Hachette UK company
www.hachetteindia.com

1

Print ISBN 978-93-5731-318-6
eBook ISBN 978-93-5731-753-5

Hachette Book Publishing India Pvt. Ltd
4th & 5th Floors, Corporate Centre,
Plot No. 94, Sector 44, Gurugram 122003, India

Typeset in Dante MT Std 12/16.5
by R. Ajith Kumar, New Delhi

Printed and bound in India
by Manipal Technologies Limited

CONTENTS

FOREWORD

Some stories hold your hand and take you for a walk. Down paths lined with mud houses of memories, past milestones that evoke pain and a sense of belonging, along roads that abruptly run into walls. Like 'The Bat'.

Some stories make you sit up and wonder if the writer was eavesdropping on your thoughts and recording your private life. Like 'Muchrindu'.

Some stories open doors and usher you into a world of harsh realities, of disturbing views. Like 'The Book Release'.

Some stories leave you craving for the good old times when there were no fences between people. Like 'Your People'.

Some stories hand you a kaleidoscope and let you play with it, and you see different shades of life every time you shake it. Like 'Recognition'.

Some stories hold a mirror to the society and its absurd

but inviolable rules, and demand it to have a look, then another look, then yet another. Like 'The Book'.

Some stories give you a compelling reason to laugh at the world, at its ways and, more importantly, laugh at yourself. Like 'A Domestic Animal'.

Some stories are nothing short of a magic carpet and you sit on its edge and have a bird's eye view of your inner self. Like 'The Genie'.

And some writers are like djinns. When they sit beside you and spin yarns, you begin to see life in a new light. Some writers like Shahina Rafiq. In this collection of surprisingly bold and amazingly well-crafted stories, she holds your hand and takes you for a long walk down a carpet woven with words.

Anees Salim

TRANSLATOR'S NOTE

Shahina Rafiq's *Menstrual Coupé: Stories* is a perfect blend of reality and imagination. Her stories are a reflection of the lived realities of women, where the world of imagination is at times the only space a woman can truly be herself, without furtively looking around to escape patriarchal policing. These stories are deeply embedded in the geo-local context of Kerala, and we as readers understand that even while the lives of women are constrained by specific cultural practices, the desire to escape patriarchal norms is pan-cultural.

The transition from the real to the imaginary is achieved with an enviable ease, as can be seen in the story titled 'The Genie'; the vocabulary used by the writer transports the reader to a liminal space where the unreal becomes real and the real unreal. Perhaps this is what a woman caught within the invisible bars of the cage erected by society does: she lives out her life mixing reality with dreams. 'Menstrual Coupé' on the other hand celebrates an exclusively female space and it is fascinating to watch different women perform their gender in completely different ways. The writer uses her narrative world to counter fascism at all levels – from the micro-space of the house to the macro-space of the nation. The stories strongly critique the different modes of fundamentalism that have crept within us. But what is remarkable is her sense of humour which laces the stories. This translation is the outcome of a harmonious collaboration with the writer. I cherished the moments we cackled with glee as we picked ourselves up after having stumbled upon certain terms that were bound to the geographic terrain of the tales.

Rafiq's language is earthy and mellifluous, and her choice of words clearly challenges existing gender norms that are followed as a matter of course. Writing and translation are intensely gendered activities. When I began to translate her stories, I paid close attention to the nuances of gender that are crucial to her stories. These stories question and challenge male assumptions about language and strive to create a literary world that is intensely female-centric but not exclusivist in nature. We hope that this book will be able to persuade readers to actively engage with a female literary imagination.

INTRODUCTION

'Hey, Sayi!'

Thus began Maimoona, while threading my hair with her fingers. Her sixth finger, just a stub that hung from the edge of her palm, touched my cheek softly.

Maimoona was married, and I was in college. While she was telling me stories (or was she talking about her own life?) the previous day, I had been playing in the backyard pond. I continued to play till my white petticoat turned brown. Nooru, Nadeera and Suleika were also there. Maimoona whitened the clothes with the white Panama soap suds. She would rub her feet on the saboon suds to whiten them. I used to think her soles were the colour of the water snake that occasionally raised its head from a corner of the pond. Once the expanse of the pond bored me, I would take a dip in the O-shaped well that had been dug in the middle of the field to water the crops. When my teeth began to chatter from the cold, I would sit beside the pond under a warm sun, ready to plunge into the water again, until Umma came for me with a stick.

Sometimes, when it rained, I would float in the pond. Echoing the water all around me, my eyes would fill with tears. My life had no scope for any existential angst. I was an only child; the younger brother would appear ten years later (he didn't create any problems then or now).

Whenever I stubbornly demanded something, my grandfather, whom I called Valyappa, would support me. I was given coconut milk with pathiri – paper-thin rice pancakes – and a deep bowl of sugar for breakfast. For lunch, I had to be given ice sticks to coax me to eat the little balls of rice Umma made with her own hands. Others washed my feet and carried me to bed as I pretended to be asleep on the bench in the kitchen. This was a snapshot of my life.

Next door to us lived two lovely people whom I called Appila and Ikkumma, names I had invented for them (my wordplay had already begun). There were no children in their house, so there were more people to pamper me. Innikutty, who used to offer me tender coconuts as I sat on the veranda swinging my legs. Chakkitkutty, Vallutty and Nadi, who used to hand me their long threshing sticks that had grown smooth from constant use as they worked in tandem to the beat of a song they sang together. I was fascinated by the long earrings that swung from Chakki's drooping ear lobes. They looked like the seeds of the sage flower. I wanted multiple piercings through the length of my ears like my grandmother, whom I called Vallimma. (That I screamed the house down when my ears were pierced is another story.) Yet I would sit alone, filled with sorrow. One needed sorrow to be able to write. And I had to write, I knew it even back then.

My school was right across from my house. I crossed the road only after the first bell rang. My religious education lasted a week. The ustad complained that my frock didn't cover my knees. Besides, I was too lazy to wake up in the morning despite the temptation of Umma's crisp achappams. My tuition classes didn't last long either. In grade four, I was put in a convent school in Malappuram where my father worked as a college teacher, and travelled to and from school on Vappa's scooter. As the scooter returned home to the welcoming golden rays of the setting sun, dragonflies with large red wings would sweep against my face, a kiss that hurt. The wind with a variety of smells would entangle itself in my hair. It carried the fragrance of the roses from the garden of the house that had figures of lions on its gate, of the pond filled with green algae, of the paddy fields that had recently been harvested and of the hay that had been stacked in a corner of a compound.

Near my school was the 'Premier Bookshop', which I often visited. I would touch and stroke the books I had decided would come home with me. I would make them my own using my pocket money. The shopkeeper would allow me to take the books home even before I paid for them. Once, in the excitement of being done with my exams, I forgot to pay him. He must have told my father when he was returning from college, so when my father came home and saw me sitting on the veranda with my legs stretched towards the areca nut tree, he asked me, 'Do you owe money to Premier Books?'

There was no anger, only a question. But as I sat, unable to meet his eyes, I vowed to make enough money to buy the Premier Bookshop and read all the books there. (I had made this promise to myself, but as it's embarrassing to ask Vappa for money to buy a bookshop, I haven't bought it yet.)

My father, who had a deep knowledge of both economics and the Quran, did not impose his will on me (I was a zero in both subjects). Instead, he gave me books to read. He presented a pocket diary with red corners to a fourth-standard student. He wrote the first line in blue ink. The mornings I woke up to the songs of K.L. Saigal and Ghulam Ali were his gifts. He showed me the sheer joy one felt while planting a sapling. In turn, Vappa was planting the seeds in me so that I could sprout.

My mother, on the other hand, was popular enough to win elections. The door to my home was always open, and the kitchen would always have food. There were very few stomachs around that hadn't been fed by Umma. Sorrow-filled eyes and hungry bellies would leave my home filled with coconut and rice, and sometimes even bangles around their wrists, which Umma lent for special occasions. I, who sat in my room hesitant to talk to people, was a zero in that department as well. Now, when I call Umma, she tells me, 'You wasted your life. Not working despite all that education. Your Vappa was saying...'

I boasted, 'Umma, tell Vappa that when you both die, your obituaries in the newspaper will say you were my parents.'

Umma would retort, 'How will I see what is written about me after I die?'

She is right. So, this book is for them. Though not of much use as a daughter, it's for them: my parents, who brought me up.

THE GENIE

The problems started after I watched a movie called *Iblis*.

Divya came home in the afternoon with her usual question, 'Have I lost weight?' We shot videos on our phones and spoke about the movie we planned to make one day. Then we went to watch *Iblis*, taking Roshni along with us: three witches to watch *Iblis*.

The popcorn and fries that we bought were mostly left uneaten. The oil had gone bad. But we enjoyed the movie. We spoke about it on our way back in the autorickshaw: the beautiful costumes in kalamkari and ikkath fabrics, and the sublime poignancy of the scene in which Fida, who had decided to die, sits on a swing. Night had fallen by the time we got home. The bouts of sneezing began after a while.

In the movie, there were scenes where people who stood next to the ghost began to sneeze. 'Has a genie entered my body?' I asked myself. 'A movie buff who has always dreamt of making a movie, but hasn't achieved anything. A corpse that sat staring at the screen even after the movie had come to an end.' I wondered whether I could write a story with these ideas. But I got bored after a while. A number of stories had been written about cinema. Even Paul Zacharia has written one!

The bouts of sneezing increased by the next day. As I listened to the torrential rainfall at night, I felt a fever creep in. I felt a piercing pain on either side of my forehead as I tried to read. I snuggled under the blanket with a couple of paracetamols inside of me. But I couldn't sleep. I woke up every hour. As I tossed and turned, I could feel the characters in the book I was reading stomping all over my head, threatening to break it open.

There is nothing more agonizing than lying awake at night. My stomach and feet started to ache as if I had menstrual cramps. I groaned each time a fresh wave of pain washed over me. If anyone outside my bedroom would hear me, they would wonder whether I had a lover inside my room when my husband was away. They would smirk upon hearing my moans.

My husband wasn't home. He would return after two weeks. His absence was an occasion for celebration. The previous day's movie was the second I had watched while he was away. My routine had changed: I slept till 9, then I made easy-to-cook dishes like dosas and boiled bananas. I warmed the leftover rice and curry I had cooked on the day he left in the microwave. When he called to find out how I was, I told him, 'It's pure bliss!'

Umma didn't like it when I gave her the same reply. 'You better watch out. It takes God very little time to deal out blows. Just see what happened…' She then proceeded to give me a list of examples. As I hung up, I wondered whether God was devoid of any sense of humour. Wouldn't he get my joke? I usually light all four burners of the stove and cook fiercely every single day. Breakfast, packed lunch with curry and stir-fried veggies – I am a lady Ravan with ten hands instead of two. Dearest God! I simply meant a break from that back-breaking schedule.

It was around 3 a.m. when I felt my stomach heave. I tasted salty fluid on my tongue. I grew nauseous and rushed to the bathroom. I vomited. My slightly protruding tummy deflated without any exercise. I woke up after 8. My mouth was dry. As I sat on the toilet taking a crap, I thought I would make a couple of dosas after. But I felt uneasy. I began to sweat, and a dark film covered my eyes. I remember standing up to get a towel. But when I opened my eyes, I was bewildered by the strange place I found myself in. I was lying flat on the bathroom floor. My lips were swollen. I had a bump on my forehead. I couldn't remember how I had fallen down. I wondered if I had washed myself before getting up.

When I told Umma about this, she took it very seriously. 'It's because you don't eat properly. Eat an egg every day, and drink milk.' For mothers, their children never grow up.

'What if something had happened?' Umma was anxious.

I would have had to come out with a broken head and call someone.

'After you are dead? Like Sainu?' Umma started with her examples.

I wanted to laugh. She was ruthlessly honest and didn't mince her words. Everyone in her family was the same. If I wore a new outfit on a festive occasion, my aunt would look at me and say, 'Is that a new dress? It isn't pretty.' I once went to her home, leaving my newly shampooed shoulder-length hair open. She told me, 'This hairstyle doesn't suit you. You look like a man who teaches Carnatic music.'

I could write a novel about her, but that will be done later. Right now, this is about the genie and me.

I like being alone; I leave my hair unbrushed and unkempt and walk around like a tigress until someone rings the bell. Sometimes I would watch them through the peephole. As the light and the shade mated under the guava tree, I wanted to set music to it. There is music in me. I don't tell you about it, but that doesn't mean it isn't there. Music is within me just like it is within a piano or a guitar. But that's not what I wanted to say. I wanted to talk about being alone. I like being alone, but when the body falls sick, one's thoughts are different. You want to rest your head against the sweaty chest of your lover who rushes in to hold you as you are about to fall. Nowadays you don't get lovers who swim across rivers to help you. They send text messages. 'Take care! Get well soon!' So let us leave them alone. A genie would do fine. Not the kind with smoke below the waist, but one with clean feet and evenly cut, well-kept toe nails.

A few days ago, a friend and I were talking about writing a novel. She said, 'What are we waiting for? Soon our eyesight will fade and our hands will falter. Shouldn't we do something before they lay us in a box?'

If she could read this, she would think, 'You are unfair, God! When she fell, she should have hit her head on the pumice stone she uses to scrub her feet, or dashed her head against the sharp end of a pipe. At least *you* should have done something, Iblis!' My friends are ruthlessly honest too.

I felt sluggish when I woke up. The feeling persisted. I had a headache at times, as if someone was tugging at my hair. I wondered whether I should go to the doctor. But the doctor was also going through a difficult time. His wife had had an aneurysm, and she was recovering after surgery. I felt bad when I saw a man look so despondent. I told him I would pray for her. As I didn't do the namaz, I thought I would talk to God when I went to bed, but my thoughts wandered and I forgot about my promise.

I thought I would use the balm my cousin had brought from Canada to soothe my headache.

'Ah! What have you done? What have you smeared on your forehead? It's hurting my eyes.'

I was stunned. Reflex action prompted me to turn around. I even looked under the bed.

'It's me, the Genie.' The voice was deep and calm.

I could dream standing up, walking or while sitting down, but I had never lost control of my senses. I was unlike other women writers who said they had experienced ecstasy or depression. I looked around.

'Despite reading *Vikram and Betaal,* don't you know where I usually sit? I don't like swinging on your hair now. It was much better when you had long, curly hair.'

No wonder I had a headache! The rascal must have been pulling on my hair since morning. I was furious.

'Why are you sitting on my shoulder? It's hurting. I don't care if you are a genie. I don't like being touched without my permission.'

There was silence for a while. Telling myself I had imagined everything, I hugged my pillow and tried to sleep.

Suddenly, the genie said, 'Shall I tell you a story?'

I couldn't see where he was. 'This is not done.'

'Do people always pay attention to you? Don't they pretend not to hear when you speak? Don't they dive into their mobile phones? Isn't that why you claim to love solitude and hide yourself inside this room?'

Oh, this genie was not bad. He had studied me in great detail.

'Well, don't startle me like you've done today. Make sure that when you come in, a fragrance warns me of your presence, a fragrance like the smell that oozes when you cut a green lime just as it is turning yellow. Or it could be music. Not the *mappila pattu* songs that one sings at Muslim weddings. Yiddish music perhaps. I like variety.'

'Didn't you dream today? That you were standing under the old sycamore in your blue-and-white uniform and waiting for the bus? Do you know why you often dream about the bus stop that is shaped like a long box?' The genie began his story.

As I lay my head on the genie's lap, I turned into the little girl who listened to her grandmother's stories. As he ran his fingers through my hair, a honeyed slumber flowed into my eyes.

'Once upon a time, there lived a prince who would get virgins to sleep with him every night.'

Hadn't my grandmother, my Ummama, told me the prince was mad? I couldn't remember.

'The very next day, he used to kill the girls.'

How did they manage to have sex with the prince while they were living the last day of their lives? But I wasn't old enough to think about this back then. Rather, I would wait eagerly for the moment when a girl would arrive with the magical flowers: three red and three blue. Every night, the girl would throw a flower at the prince, who would immediately fall asleep. This went on for six nights, and on the seventh morning, the prince woke up cured of his madness. He then married the girl and they lived happily ever after.

Are beautiful virgins meant to be given to mad, violent men? Perhaps women suffer because they cannot tell stories like Scheherazade could. I've never heard a story where a male virgin was given to an insane princess. I decided to ask Genie. But by the time I woke up from my flower-induced slumber, he had vanished. I thought I would ask him the next day. But he did not appear for two days. Though I had known him only for a short while, his absence enveloped me like a nameless sorrow. I went crazy when I remembered him running his fingers through my hair, listening to my mad chatter and talking to me. As the twilight sky burnt orange, darkness descended on me. I felt like listening to sad songs and crying. I slid into a deep sleep.

The pond was filled with waterweeds and shikakai leaves. Small fish and silvery minnows swam across shaking their tails. I sniffed at a shikakai bud, but didn't eat it thinking of the sweet-and-sour aftertaste it left in the mouth. It was then that the child came towards me and extended her dirty hands towards my white frock that Umma had washed till it sparkled.

I woke up on hearing footsteps in my room. Genie sat on the doorstep. I don't know why I cried, but I hugged him and told him the child's name was Unkuvava. Genie held me close and kissed my forehead. He started singing:

Then, in the year nineteen twenty-one,
We fought the whites together, here in Kerala,
Where the valiant sons of Eranad shed their blood;
The brave Variyan Kunnath Kunjahammed Haji
And his troops fought like warring cockerels.
Fathers, uncles, and elder uncles from beyond Kozhikode,
All of them fought;
And how many villains had we sent to the gallows then,
For their debauchery towards our mothers and sisters.
And elders were tortured;
Their beards were shaved, needles driven into their toes.
Some were taken prisoners
and were deported
To the Andamans, beyond the sea.

At Mongam, a few miles from Mancheri,
Live valiant and patriotic souls.
*Whites, you better run back to England with your dear lives.**

---

* The Mappila Rebellion of 1921 occurred in the Eranad and Velluvanadan districts of present-day Kerala, when the Mappila peasants revolted against the British colonial administration and local landlords.

Though he sang well, I changed the track to my favourite Hindi songs in my mind. He might have sensed it as he stopped humming.

'The song is nice. What film is it from?' I asked.

'Consciousness and conviction are needed.'

He went silent after that.

'How are genies and the Iblis related? Are you cousins? Why is everyone afraid of the Iblis? You are very friendly,' I asked him, changing the subject.

'Everyone wants passive acceptance, but those who ask questions turn into Satan, Iblis, Maoist or Feminichi*.'

I liked that philosophy.

'Do you know that you were born in a country which used to banish women to the Andaman Islands if they dared to question the system? Yet you float around, without a sense of history or knowledge about your roots.'

'Aren't the Andaman Islands a nice place? I have always wanted to spend a few days there, eating seafood and relaxing.'

Genie went away as if in response to a call. I felt he had a fetish for history. Men usually have the habit of saying women have no sense of history or politics, so I started to do a bit of research. Google, and friends in the media, helped me. Well, despite Genie's claims, I could find no information about women being banished to the Andamans. But women had accompanied their husbands

---

* A slur for feminists.

to the islands. There were places in the Andamans called Manjeri and Vandoor that were similar to places in Malappuram. I also discovered the history of a bus stop in Malappuram.

The bus stop at Valluvambram Junction had been built after demolishing the Hitchcock Memorial. A single-minded resistance launched by the people of Eranad brought down the memorial erected in the name of Hitchcock, a British police officer who led a brutal attack on Muslims during the 1921 Malabar revolt.

That day, Genie sang a battle song written by Kambalath Govindan Nair. The song was about the Malabar revolt and its aftermath.

The rebels had stoned Hitchcock to death. The British then built a memorial in his name in Valluvambram. The movement against the British gained strength in 1944. People from different lands marched to Valluvambram singing the song written by Govindan Nair. The communist leader A.K. Gopalan, also known as AKG, and Mohammed Abdur Rahiman Sahib also participated in the struggle. Though I managed to gather these details, I still could not connect my dream about the bus stop to this incident. The song says the memorial was built in a nearby place called Mongam. In any case, the majority only needed a statue for birds to shit on and reinvent their historical consciousness.

When Genie came to me the next day, I showed off

my newly acquired knowledge. 'When you can Google it, why should you bother to read history? I never liked the subject anyway. When I was in school…'

'When the globe fell over, you laughed and the teacher made you write a thousand lines as punishment. You've hated the subject since then, I know. I read your Facebook post.'

My jaw dropped. I felt as if my clothes had been stripped off. As I wondered how I would touch myself without being seen, Genie said, 'I'm a genie, not a human. I don't invade anyone's privacy.'

That night, I dreamt of Genie. We were climbing a hill covered in trees. I didn't feel tired at all, maybe because he held my hand. When we reached the top of the hill, there was a flat and open grassland where light mingled with the green. As I lay on my back gazing at the sky, Genie lay down beside me. As I rested my head on his shoulders, my feminine envy wounded me with the thought that a number of women may have laid their heads on his chest. Suddenly, my hand touched a hole in his chest. Why hadn't I noticed this before? Did God take away the hearts of genies? I pressed my face to the hole.

'Genie, can you give me this space? I want to put my stories, my love and my madness inside.'

He held me tight till I almost suffocated. My question, about whether he would always be with me, was lost in the tightness of his embrace.

My days began to revolve around Genie. I told him every single thing I knew or had experienced.

'Genie, why did you tell me something that never happened? Women were never banished from here.'

'What sort of a writer are you? Imagine you are a schoolgirl with your hair in braids, waiting at the bus stop. A girl comes to you, wearing a kaachi,* a blouse, a veil and anklets. Walk towards the past with her and see the world through her eyes. Imagine the passive acceptance, the resistance, the exodus and the pain she must have suffered. Suppose she had a lover and they banished him to the Andamans? Isn't that deep enough to write a novel?'

Genie was on fire. The girl's face took shape in my mind. I saw the bus stop in sepia and could hear her anklets. Did they have gold beads inside them? Had she fallen in love with a man from a different religion? I didn't know much about the religious practices that existed then. I needed to do more research. It was an age and a culture that needed to be marked.

I asked him, 'Well, seeing that you know it so well, why don't you write the novel for me?'

That was the night Genie disappeared.

---

* A dhoti worn by Muslim women.

A DOMESTIC ANIMAL

I.

The jingle about the cow screamed from the TV over and over. Spandana wanted to push the TV off the stand and smash it open. As she ran towards it in a fit of rage and switched it off, her daughter who had planted herself in front of the TV began to scream. She slapped the child and returned to the curry cooking on the stove. She had put more salt than was needed, so she sliced a potato in half and dropped it into the pot. She simmered in anger along with the curry.

She felt guilty at having vented her ire towards Varun ettan on her child, so Spandana went back to the living room. The child lay on the floor sucking her thumb. She was still whimpering. Spandana carried her to the kitchen, put her on the table, and gave her a bit of jaggery to suck on. She removed the child's frock and rubbed coconut oil on her. The child had rashes all over. After bathing her in lukewarm water, Spandana applied the ointment the doctor had prescribed. Leaving the child to play, she picked up the phone to call her mother. Then she decided not to. Neither her father nor her mother understood her plight. 'Stop whining. He's a nice man,' was their constant refrain. So she dialled Yamini instead, praying that her phone wouldn't be engaged as usual.

II.

'Can I come over?'

'Wat 4?'

'To stay 4 a couple of days.'

'Come.'

'Wat wil ur mum say?'

'She won't mind.'

'Isnt ur room upstairs?'

'Ya.'

'Then its ok. Is there a bathroom upstairs?'

'You'd need it only after the mass.'

Isa sent back the smirking face emoticon. It took a while for the smile to reach Yamini's face.

'You rogue!' She added a throbbing red heart.

'I'm feeling greedy.'

……

'R u there? R u chatting with someone else?'

'Chechi is calling me.'

'What's up?'

'The cow problem.'

'Oh! Your "common mother"!'

And for you it's the pig, mumbled Yamini to herself. 'Wl u come? Let's go 4 a drive.'

'I can't even kiss u in that place. Cm to Kochi. Wl take an OYO.'

'That's not safe. She's calling again I've to go.'

'Who knows which chechi is calling u.'

Yamini didn't attend to the call nor did she type a reply to Isa. She thought to herself, 'Chechi was never like this before.'

III.

Spandana realized she could not control her anger. Yesterday, she had even fought with Varun ettan's father. Yesterday was a horrible day. She hadn't even changed out of her sari after getting back from school. The woman who looked after her child had asked for an advance of ₹2,000. She had taken out the money from her bag, thinking the nanny was making it a habit to ask for an advance.

It was then that she heard a commotion outside. Her daughter ran out calling, 'Acha'. She was surprised to find he had returned early from the bank. As she went to the veranda, she walked into a crowd. She withdrew upon seeing so many unfamiliar faces. As Varun ettan asked her to make tea, a chorus of voices went up saying, 'No, we don't want tea. It's okay.'

She didn't know how she would produce so many cups and saucers at such short notice, so she went to bathe. When she came out wearing a nightie, she saw the cow in the front yard. A brown cow with a white mark on its forehead. Her daughter danced around the cow, while Varun ettan stood straight, glowing like the evening sun.

IV.

'That was a good move,' Nair sir said the moment he saw Spandana in the morning.

'You don't tell us anything and expect us to find out from the papers?' Ancy was envious.

In response to Saira's query, 'Do you have enough space?' another colleague Sujatha's voice flamed into Spandana's ears, 'Oh, she thinks we don't have a large compound or a big house like she does.'

Saira must have heard her. 'I asked if you have space only because you live in town.' She dived back into the pages of her book.

Spandana wanted to say, *Seven cents of land is enough for a cow. People even grow vegetables on their terrace now.*

But as the 'Jana Gana Mana' pealed from the mike, she swallowed her words and stood up. When she remembered her first class was with 10C, she discarded all thoughts of the cow.

'What are the chemical reactions that oxygen produces on the surfaces of metals? What are the elements that quicken the process?' Spandana looked around expectantly, hoping at least one of her students would answer.

Surprisingly, someone from the back bench stood up.

'Teacher, you will get enough oxygen now, won't you?'

'You can use cow urine to make tea!'

'Shut up, you anti-national!'

Spandana shouted over the cacophony, 'Silence!'

V.

Binutha arrived at the bank earlier than usual. Work was hectic; admissions to professional colleges were ongoing, and many had come to the bank for loans. They had unending doubts, and once she sat in her seat, she would become too busy to even move.

She sat next to Varun nowadays. He smelled lovely. She wondered which perfume he used. He was also well-dressed and groomed himself. She had noticed how clean his feet were when he had worn open sandals on a rainy day. Making love to him must be a beautiful experience, she thought with a tinge of desire. She quickly exonerated herself. It was only a thought.

Just as she wondered why Varun was late that day,

he entered, looking a bit dishevelled. By then, her first customer had arrived.

Binutha didn't know why everyone had surrounded Varun during lunchtime. It was Shinto who showed her the newspaper.

A cow!

Binutha turned from the paper and looked at Varun in surprise.

VI.

'Where do we build the cow shed?'

There was little space behind the kitchen. Spandana wanted to build a bathroom for the maid, but there wasn't enough space even to dig a compost pit for the garbage. The well was in the front of the house. Spandana treasured her green patch near the well. But when she returned from school, she saw that the cow had wrecked her well-maintained garden. She immediately called Varun. Luckily for him, he had been too busy to answer the call. But when he reached home, Spandana's sharp gaze greeted him.

'Let's put the flower pots on the wall. That will give us some space. Cow dung is an excellent fertilizer.'

The cow had dropped its dung in circles all over the lawn. Varun thought it would be good to pour water over it and spread it across the lawn. He also expected her clichéd retort: 'Why don't you smear it on your head as well?'

But he hadn't expected her to give him the silent treatment for so many days.

A few people came home to enquire.

'Where do we build the cow shed?'

'You must build it soon. How can you make her stand in the sun the entire day? Would you have done this to your mother?'

Though they were smiling, they spoke a different language from the corners of their eyes. From then onwards, the cow entered the car shed, while the car was parked outside. Spandana, who used to leave her bedroom window facing the front yard open, closed it. Varun did not stop her as the pair of eyes that now shone outside the window seemed quite uncomfortably human.

VII.

The champa flower she had tucked in her hair and tied into a bun was fragrant. A butterfly was poised for flight below her left shoulder. His hands reached to untie the string that held her blouse together and fondle the twins.

'Varun etta!'

He stretched his hands to hold her closer.

'Get up!'

Spandana was shaking him awake. When did she get a butterfly tattoo?

'The champa flowers?' He looked at her hair.

'What flower! Get out of bed, someone has come to meet you.' She glanced over her shoulder with a threat hidden in her eyes.

What a dream that was. What would Spandana have thought? Who was that woman? He couldn't see her face. As he thought about her smooth back, it took him a while to urinate.

'Moo!'

Reality's siren woke him up from his reverie. He put on a shirt and went out.

'Sur ettan said you need someone to take care of the cow.'

'Yes, you have to feed and wash her and get rid of its dung.'

'Do you have space behind the house?'

'No,' said Varun. 'I forgot to ask you your name.'

'Karun C. Nair.'

'Do you have a lot of land in your hometown?'

'Oh no! I live in a flat here.'

Varun felt the cow had chewed up the sapling of hope that had sprouted in his mind. And when he heard the wages the man demanded, he thought it would be better if he resigned from his job at the bank and took up this work himself. He could see their family budget going haywire. As Varun debated whether to tell the man to come twice a week, Spandana summoned him.

'Tell him to finish his work by eight in the morning.'

'Why?'

Spandana looked at him in a way that said his head was filled with cow dung.

'Do you know him well? Who he is and where he stays?'

Varun shook his head.

'Both of us leave for work by 8.30. Your father spends most of his time in bed. Who else is here? Vasanthi chechi, this man, this house and my daughter. I want to go to work in peace.'

'His demands are unreasonable. Shall we give Vasanthi chechi some extra money and ask her to look after the cow as well?'

'Her? She is too lazy to bathe the child or give Achan his medicines. In fact, I was thinking of sending her away when the little one goes to school in June.'

When Varun walked out, Karun was clicking a selfie with the cow.

'It's for Instagram.'

'You must come by seven in the morning. You will have to bathe the cow, feed it and get rid of the dung.'

'At seven? I go to bed only by 2 a.m. The dung? I guess Chechi and you will have to start drying it by sticking it on your compound's wall as they do in Tamil Nadu.' He laughed at his own joke.

Varun brooded about the situation at home while at work. He called Spandana.

'Babe, your parents have a huge compound in their house. Shall we keep the cow there till we settle things?'

'Good idea. My father has just had a bypass surgery and my mother constantly complains of aching knees. Let us buy an ox as well.' She disconnected the call without waiting for his reply.

Varun felt that she was now the husband and he the wife in their marriage. She came from Kannur, the land of rebellions. Stereotypically, she resisted everything and walked around thinking she was always right.

Spandana had gone to the veranda to speak to Varun. Sujatha was in the staff room; the nosy woman would want to know all the details about her call. Spandana felt she could not get any peace of mind anywhere. She thought about whether she should go to her parents' house for a while. She began to smile thinking about spending some quality sister-time chatting with Yamini. It was then that the rascal from 10C asked her, 'Did you find anyone to milk the cow?'

She felt his eyes crawling over her chest like a worm that couldn't be shaken off.

The students were on strike, and classes were suspended earlier than usual that day. Spandana was relieved. Her feet rushed to go as far away from the students and the campus as possible. She heaved a sigh when she hopped on to the first bus and grabbed a seat. She looked out and realized she hadn't seen these sights in a long time.

When she opened the gate to her home, the cow was sleeping in the car shed. 'Amma,' her daughter, who was playing in the lawn, called out. Cow dung clung to her body and clothes. Spandana felt a tremor inside her. Placing her bag in the veranda, she tucked her sari in and hosed down her daughter, and took her to the bathroom to bathe her thoroughly.

Vasanthi chechi was dozing on the sofa in the sitting room. Hearing the child's screams, she woke up and looked embarrassed when she saw Spandana, who told her, 'Chechi, go home if you want.' She pretended not to hear when Vasanthi murmured, 'How long can I lock up the child inside the house?' She felt jealous of her father-in-law who had descended into a world of lost memories.

The smell of meat rolls wafted in from Hamid Ikka's house. Spandana felt hungry, both in her mind and her body. She had to talk to someone to unburden herself. She picked up the child, locked the door, and went to Hamid's house. Hamid Ikka's daughter Mahima was younger than Varun by a few years. She was married and had settled down in New Zealand. Both she and her husband were doctors. She remembered they had gone shopping the last time Mahima had come to India. *When will she come next?* Spandana wondered.

When she rang the bell, Hamid Ikka opened the door.

'Did you return early today?'

'Student strike, Hamid-ka. Classes were let off early.'

'Sit. Maaji, look, Spandana is here.'

Hamid-ka lifted the little girl and swung her. 'What a

nice dress you are wearing,' he said. He asked Spandana about her work.

'What are you doing, Maaji? We have guests, but where is the tea?'

'Am I a guest?' Spandana asked, and walked towards the kitchen. Maaji came out with a cup of tea and a plate of chips. Putting it on the table, she closed the kitchen door. 'The exhaust fan isn't working. The kitchen is filled with smoke.'

The child grabbed some chips and ran around. Hamid Ikka ran after her in a playful mood.

Spandana felt her hunger and urge for conversation subside. She asked them about Mahima and made a few cursory comments about the maid. Then she got up to leave. 'Achan must have woken up. I must give him tea.' She prepared to leave, telling herself she must have been mistaken about the meat rolls.

Hamid shut the door and asked his wife, 'Why didn't you give them the meat rolls? The child loves it.'

'They have one in their front yard. Let them take a piece and cook it. I don't want to be accused of feeding them beef.' Majida returned to the kitchen.

Hamid thought about an incident from two days ago. A boy had been coming to Varun's house to take care of the cow. Their next-door neighbour, Dr Indira, had two grown-up daughters, and the boy paraded his muscular body while bathing the animal. He always left the hose on, and the water flowed to Hamid's low-lying compound and formed a puddle with a foul smell.

When Maaji stood at their gate and told him off, the boy looked at Hamid and said, 'Do you want to go to Pakistan?'

VIII.

'Varun etta, this won't work. The boy never comes on time. I had to take two half-days off just because he came late to milk the cow. You don't have any leave. You pay him so much, and for what? What does he do? He doesn't even clean up the dung. You should see the backyard. It is filled with insects and flies. The house smells like a cowshed now. I don't know when the neighbours will start complaining. What is wrong with you?'

'Cow – oxy…'

Varun stopped, fearing an explosion if Spandana's gaze met the word 'oxygen'.

He too was fed up of cleaning up on the days when Karun didn't turn up for work. But he didn't complain and tried to convince himself it made for good exercise. His daily routine had gone awry. Before the cow had arrived, he would lie in bed in the morning, hugging his daughter till Spandana brought him a cup of tea. He had a morning routine: watch strident right-wing channels, take a leisurely bath and get ready for office. Now, he had to wake up early, spray water on the cow, take it out to the lawn, then clean the shed. The dung had to be put in the pit dug behind the kitchen. Once, he saw Teena and Reena, the girls next door, look at him in disgust. After that, he would wake up early and finish the chores before anyone could see him. His sleep pattern had been disturbed, and he would be tired after all the physical labour. His work at the bank suffered too. He felt his eyes closing while he tallied accounts. Even Binutha looked at him disparagingly now. Binutha, who was polite and always smiled at him when they spoke (his friends had even teased him about her). But the previous day, she looked at him as if he made her nauseous. She got up from her seat. He followed her glance and saw that cow dung was stuck between the toes on his left foot, and even under his nails. He couldn't believe it. How had he missed it?

After scrubbing his feet clean that night, he sat on the sofa and googled 'Pampers for Pets.'

IX.

Spandana was caught in a dreamless sleep. It was tiring, to work both at school and at home, and then take care of the child too. She fell asleep the moment her head touched the pillow. Then she heard a groan, and felt someone's touch. She thought she was dreaming and did not open her eyes. She felt someone twitching near her. She woke up with a start. Her child was tossing and turning, her body hot.

Spandana got up and turned on the light. The child was gasping for breath. There were rashes all over her body. The mother in her felt as if her soul was burning. She screamed, and Varun woke up. Taking turns, they carried the child on their shoulder, trying to calm her down. They tried to make her drink water. They shook off the bed cover thinking an insect may have crawled over her. But the child wouldn't stop crying. Her back began to bend like a bow. It was three in the morning, but they had to get the child to a doctor. In desperation, they went to Dr Indira's home and rang the bell.

As the doctor examined the child, she asked them, 'Did she have fever in the morning?'

'No, she was perfectly alright this morning.'

'I will give her something that will bring the fever down. I think it's an allergic reaction. But we must consult a paediatrician. You can come with me to the hospital in the morning.'

Varun and Spandana wanted to apologize for having woken the doctor up so early, but she had already closed the door.

Once back home, they didn't sleep. They carried the child in turns and promised offerings to their personal gods.

X.

'She is wheezing. Did she do it before?'

'No.'

'Does anyone at home have asthma or wheezing?'

'No.'

'What did she eat for dinner?'

'Rice gruel.'

'Did she eat anything from outside yesterday? Hotel food or packed juice?'

'No.'

Spandana replied in the negative to Dr Raghunath's questions, but she wondered if Vasanti chechi had fed her something. The doctor examined the child thoroughly, who lay limp, tired from all the crying.

'Do you have pets?'

'No' she said. Varun interrupted her, 'We have a cow.'

'Is the cow shed near the house?'

'We don't have a cow shed.'

The doctor stopped examining the child and looked at them.

Varun explained the situation.

The doctor said, 'Look, cows have fleas on them. And if the cow isn't bathed properly, the fleas multiply. Nowadays crows and mynahs don't feed off the insects from the cows as they used to. The child has developed an allergy because of her proximity to the animal. That is why she has been wheezing. You must understand that medicines alone won't do the trick. Wash her clothes and the bed sheet in warm water. But be very careful. She's just a child.'

While Varun went to call an auto, Spandana went to meet Dr Indira.

'Spandana, I have been meaning to speak to you,' Dr Indira told her. 'We can't even open the windows that face your house. The smell is very bad. My kitchen is infested with insects and flies. Reena and Teena's friends don't come home these days. Please don't feel bad, but we have been facing a lot of difficulties. That boy is also a nuisance. Please understand that I am a mother to two teenage daughters.' The displeasure on her face was quite evident.

When they returned home, Varun's father was sitting in the veranda. His dhoti was wet. Varun took him inside and cleaned him up. He also changed the bed sheets. Spandana remembered she hadn't given him any food. Handing the child to the maid, she went to the kitchen.

They heard Karun's bike enter the porch. It was past 10 a.m.

'Haven't I told you to come early?' Varun asked him.

He hadn't expected Varun to be home at that time of the day.

'Why don't you install a punching machine?'

Varun lost his temper. He told Karun not to bother to come if he couldn't come early.

Karun spat back, 'You can't do that after entrusting me with the job. I don't care if you are the boss. You better talk politely. If you don't, I will upload a video on Facebook saying you are ill-treating the *gaumata*. Then see what happens.'

He revved up his bike and drove off.

XI.

On the second day that Spandana was absent from school, she received a call from the principal.

'If you don't come to school, the children will suffer. Their exams are approaching. They tell me you have a lot to cover. If the pass percentage is low, the school won't get the required number of students for the next academic year.'

Spandana didn't even listen to the last part of the conversation. She dialled Yamini and sobbed, 'You have to come over. The little one is ill. Come for two days at least.'

Yamini did not attend the afternoon classes. Instead she went home and packed a bag. She did not tell her parents the child was ill as they would worry. She called Isa once she got on the bus.

'I'm going to Chechi's house.'

'Why? You never told me.'

'Her child is ill, and she's very upset. I am on my way now.'

'Where are you?'

'I am on the bus.'

'Oh! You couldn't find time to message me.'

'I had to leave suddenly.'

'You are always in a hurry. When I want to meet you, you tell me that you have classes, practical tests...'

'Why don't you try to understand my situation?'

'Carry on then.'

Isa disconnected the call and then refused to answer when she called back. Yamini felt it wasn't easy to be in love.

XII.

Eleven missed calls. Yamini's heart missed a beat. Isa hadn't answered her calls the previous day. She knew he could be stubborn, so she had continued to call him, muttering to herself whatever she wanted to tell him.

Isa answered finally.

'What were you up to in the morning?'

'I was helping Chechi in the kitchen. Varun ettan was bathing the cow so I helped him hose it down and clean the shed. Then I got soaked, so I went for a bath. The phone was charging, so I didn't hear it ring.' Yamini tried to recollect all that she had done so far in the right order.

'Where is your sister?'

'She's gone to school.'

'And the child?'

'She is sleeping. She ran a high fever last night.'

'Varun?'

'He is getting ready to go to work.'

'Were you on all fours?'

Yamini didn't understand at first. Then, when the sharpness of the words struck her, she writhed as if someone had slapped her.

'Isa, mind your words.'

'Why should I? You people are notorious cheaters. Your women, who had many liaisons, used to leave a mattress out for the men, remember?'

'Even then it doesn't match up to the Immaculate Conception.'

They tore apart three-and-a-half years of love with words.

XIII.

Spandana had thought of conceiving another child during the cool rains of July. If it was a boy, he would be named Amay, meaning 'night rain', and Ameya if it was a girl. If the due date was in mid-April, she could continue teaching till March 31, when the summer vacations began. She could rejoin on the 1st of June, then take maternity leave till December 31. If she took leave without pay, she could even stay at home till next year's summer vacation. The child would turn one by then and she wouldn't have to teach with painfully engorged breasts. She could ask her mother to stay with them for some time. The older one would start school by then…

Spandana thought about the plans she and Varun had made as she sat by herself in the staffroom during the first period after lunch. They had calculated everything, but now they didn't even touch each other, or have a proper conversation. She felt gloomy. Yamini's presence was comforting and she felt relieved when they chatted once she got back from work. She tried to ignore Yamini when she said the cow hadn't eaten all day and had bellowed often.

The child slept with Yamini. Spandana shaved her underarms and her triangle. She had a leisurely oil bath. She came to the bedroom leaving her hair open. It was only when their lips met that she realized how hungry she was. She held his stone-hard greed in her palm. For a moment they debated whether to use protection or not. But the moment they decided they didn't want to use one, the cow bellowed and pushed its horns through the window. Varun drew back, now shrivelled. Spandana realized why the cow was bellowing so much.

'Go fuck the cow!' She opened the cupboard and threw a packet of condoms at Varun in rage. 'Use it. I don't want to play midwife to the cow.'

Putting on her nightdress, she left the room.

XIV.

The cow continued to bellow all day and night. Varun and Spandana could not even look at their neighbours. 'This is madness,' Yamini declared before leaving.

Varun knew the cow would stop bellowing only if he got it mated. A calf! Double the shit! Bathing both mother and child! He felt his head grow numb. As he lay awake, he remembered a story he had studied in school or college. A cow had been killed by feeding it a lump of jaggery with a hidden needle. Wasn't the cow named Gora? But who had written the story?

As he wondered why he had thought of that particular story, he fell asleep.

XV.

Varun screamed loudly.

He had been kicked in the belly. He groaned with pain and held his stomach. The ball of jaggery lay scattered. It began to hurt each time he pissed, and his urine was tinged with blood.

Then one midnight, Varun walked out without making any noise. His stomach still hurt. Untying the cow, he led it out to the main road. He thought to himself he would leave the cow in the open ground next to where the municipality dumped its garbage. Just then, it began to bellow and refused to move. He tugged at the rope and the cow mooed louder.

Varun was quite unaware of the crowd that was gathering behind him.

THE BOOK

The first words that sprung to Anitha's mind were, 'You deserve it!' But she couldn't say that to someone who had come to her seeking a counsellor's help.

'I never thought my own Pathu would do this to me.'

'What about the things you did to her, Mustafa?'

Mustafa bowed his head in response to Anitha's question. It was a question he had asked himself several times. He had said it in a fit of anger. But he hadn't imagined it would all lead to this.

'Is there a way out, Ustad?'

'Why couldn't you have stopped after saying it once?'

The day had begun badly for Mustafa. He had woken up to the warm trickle of his younger son Fazil's pee. According to the holy law, he was now unclean, and had to bathe before going to the mosque for the subahi prayers. But he didn't want to draw water from the well and bathe in the lashing rain, so he asked his wife, Pathu, to heat some water for him.

'Oh, you have stacked wooden logs here, haven't you? My mouth has become dry begging you for a gas stove. I must be the only person in this neighbourhood who has to blow into the fire to cook.' Pathu spat fire at him.

Without bathing, Mustafa changed his dhoti and went to a nearby tea stall. The smoky tea reminded him of his unpaid bills. His vehicle was rarely hired out these days. The engine needed to be repaired as well. But he sat nonplussed. When he got home, Pathu and their daughter were having a fight. Mustafa wanted to slap Muthu, who was insisting on a new umbrella to take to school. The fight ended with him saying *talaq, talaq, talaq*.

The Ustad stroked his white beard.

'If you had said it just once, you could have taken her back.'

'Can't you do something? It's not that I don't love her. After all, she gave birth to both my children.'

'How can I do something that is not in the Book, Mustafa?'

'But…'

'Don't worry. We can find a way out. After all, we have people to help us in such a predicament. We will get Pathu married to Hassan Mullah and ask him to divorce her the very next day. Then you can take her back.'

Mustafa couldn't sleep the night Hassan married Pathu. He climbed the roof of Hassan's house, removed a tile and peeked inside. He couldn't believe what he saw. He had seen such things only in English movies! Was that his Pathu lying down and then sitting up writhing in pleasure?

'I remarried her. But I can't get that image out of my mind,' he sobbed to Anitha.

Meanwhile, Pathu had come home with a new Quran that she had bought from the five hundred rupees she had received as alimony.

MUCHRINDU

Dear God! I don't like these women. I have never used foul language, because my faith forbids it.

Yet, today, I had to use cuss words because of this girl who has a crush on my man.

'A little romance would be cool. Hugs would be nice. Free sex would be nicer…'

Her English buggery! And this idiot shows me all the messages he gets. He knows I am getting marriage proposals. He also knows I am still confused as to whether we should get married or not. Why would I not be worried? If we have a child, it would be a *Muchrindu*, a Muslim-Christian-Hindu crossbreed. If a boy, I could get him circumcised by telling them he can't pee properly. If a girl, I could hope she falls in love with someone from our own religion and then call herself Aisha or Fathima and thus find her way to heaven. Merciful Allah! You are my only refuge.

It is a blessing that my would-be father-in-law is a Christian and mother-in-law a Hindu. I wouldn't have to go for confession. How on earth could I confess I had lied about going on a study tour and instead spent the day with him? I laughed as I imagined myself telling the priest, 'Oh Father! The fragrance of his sweat is intoxicating!'

The two angels on my shoulders keep an account of everything I do. I had no doubts that both the angels, Munkar and Nakir, would come with my report card on judgment day. But I was sure that my nikah would be with him only, even though he is a *Chrindu*.

Here comes another message from that bitch! 'Sometimes I feel that these "mofos" must be taught that women can happily live alone.'

He grinned from ear to ear, saying, 'Mofos is a nice word. I am hearing it for the first time.'

I made up my mind to teach him one page from the dictionary every day once we got married. I felt an uncontrollable rage creep in from my toes. 'Was the bitch in heat? Why does she want my man?' I burst out in fury.

'You are growing younger by the day, both in body and mind. I haven't gone with her, have I? Why are you so angry then?'

This is a typical male strategy, to tell women they look younger every day. I was about to explode, but then...

When his moustache brushed against my cheek, I became wet. I had lost my veil somewhere. When he held me tight, I could feel my heart melt in his heat. As I kissed him beneath his earlobe, I heard a voice say, 'You are with a Kafir. Don't you want to go to heaven, sister?'

Is there another heaven?

YOUR PEOPLE

Jo called me to find out whether I had reworked the script. But I hadn't even opened it.

A bulbul had made its nest in my writing room. I was wary about turning on the fan in case it hit her while she flew to the nest. My presence did not worry her, but I felt that she needed some privacy.

'Well, if you get time after taking care of your new admirers, do start writing.'

I could sense the detritus of our quarrel in his words. The thing is, he wanted to make a movie set in Mexico, but I didn't find the story interesting enough, and I told him so. When he asked me to think about it, I blurted out, 'Why should I? It's not my screenplay.'

'You do what benefits you. You are right. One should learn from you.'

This is why I have a problem with words. They are like water. Just as water takes the shape of the vessel it is poured into, words change their meaning depending on the mental state of the listener.

I could counter him in two ways:

1. 'Is this what you think of me? I am hurt.' (Thus, using the armour of emotions.)

2. Shout at him. (Turn aggressive so that he would not be able to say anything.)

But I prefer a third way. When words hurt my oversized ego, I lock up my anger and hurt and brood over them. I turn silent, like walking inside a factory that is no longer in operation. It is scary, but intriguing to travel further inside, dust down old sorrows, and brush away the cobwebs spun over them.

But I exaggerate. Nothing as drastic happened. I hate admitting defeat. Before disconnecting the call, Jo had told me a one-liner story that a new scriptwriter had narrated. It was a tale of revenge. I wondered why I could not think of a similar plot earlier. I need to watch more Hollywood movies.

A story then took over my mind: a story about a surgeon and his family. Mammootty, the aging superstar, would be ideal for the role of the surgeon. The tall and slim Sumalatha would fit the role of his wife. They used to make a good on-screen pair. Nazriya would be perfect as the twenty-year-old daughter who was doing MBBS – she had an innocent charm, but who knew whether she would come back to movies? The heroine wasn't important. She just needed to have a pretty face. But would Mammootty agree to act as the father of a 22-year-old?

I got into the auto carrying the burden of these thoughts while on my way towards the netherworld of my girlfriends.

It was a half-an-hour ride to Amuda's home.

'Have you fallen in love after marriage?'

I was meeting Amuda after many days. Her eyes told me she had gotten into some sort of a tangle. This girl, I tell you! She is my friend, although we don't agree on most things. She is also ruthlessly honest. She is unconcerned about her audience when she speaks. But as I was not inclined to such brutal honesty, I changed the topic.

We discussed the script we had planned to write together. We laughed our guts out imagining a scenario where we would choose a Bollywood hunk as the hero and pin him down on the casting couch. It was late when I left her place. That night, she sent me a long note:

'There is a languor when I vomit or when they give me an epidural. It is a pleasurable state, I feel my limbs have faded away. I think I experienced the greatest pleasure of my life when they gave me a spinal injection before the caesarean operation. It was better than an orgasm – just a prick as I felt my veins tearing apart from pain. I vomited today as well. It was indigestion. I thought I would be a chaste wife, but I was wrong. Like most marriages, our relationship changed too, and we became more like siblings. To look sexy, one has to put on an act. But how can you act in front of someone who knows you so well? It was then that I met him. I felt the spark you get when you touch someone inadvertently. Both of us realized it. After that, I couldn't bear the husband's touch. You know, because you can only love one at a time. Our extramarital affair was confined to just a kiss. What a nasty term – 'extramarital affair'! After a long time, I became wet during a telephone conversation. It was sheer pleasure, but I felt guilty. It is not by having sex that one cheats; it is when one gets emotionally involved with another. I pushed my fingers into my mouth and puked out the indigestion.'

I felt Amuda would have sent the note to her husband as well. That is how she is. I told her I would turn this into a story. She sent me two smileys.

When I finished reading Amuda's note, a new character developed in my mind: the doctor's assistant, a handsome young man, a bit of an introvert and quite bright. An expert surgeon: Manu. The doctor's daughter has a crush on him.

Late evening: The doctor and his wife are watching TV and chatting. Their daughter, Veni, walks down the stairs. She goes into the dining room and drinks water. Then she comes in and sits down, leafing through a magazine. She changes the channel. She has something to say, but her parents pretend not to notice.

Veni speaks nonetheless, 'My exams are from next month. I am thinking of moving to the hostel. I have a lot to study and it is easier to go to the library from the hostel.'

Her father nods. But Veni has more to say. She tries to tell them about something funny that happened in class, but the joke falls flat. She decides to leave the room. As she gets up, her father says, 'Manu said he wants to come over with his parents next Sunday. I told them to come after your exams.'

Her mother stifles her laughter.

Veni's face reflects her swiftly changing expressions. Her face is on screen in a close-up shot.

'Neither of you is fated to be surprised.'

She goes to her room and shuts the door. The doctor and his wife smile at each other. Veni falls on her bed. She blushes, a coy smile on her face. A song sequence may follow.

I tried to imagine their romance. I wanted a few scenes at least that were not clichéd. I pretended to be Veni as I floated through a daydream. As I was about to put rice into the boiling water, I realized that I had run out of rice. It was like an interval. I had to pause my thoughts midway. I put on a pair of jeans and a kurta and went to the nearby supermarket. As I dropped a couple of biscuits and munchies into my shopping cart, I saw an old classmate with whom I had studied journalism. I hadn't seen him in ages. He had put on a lot of weight. As we talked about things past and present, I told him I liked the colour of his shirt – an apple-green shirt. 'Of course, you would! Your people have an affinity for this colour,' he said. I saw the multi-coloured threads around his wrist and the sandalwood paste on his forehead. I excused myself and left.

When I got home, I noticed my plants were drooping. As it had been cloudy the previous day, I hadn't watered them. It had so far been a monsoon that showered sunshine.

'All the green shall perish,' warned my inner voice, which increased my sense of angst. Such things should be represented in movies, I felt. But who would want to watch such movies? I thought of a new character: Mohini. She filled the script in the first half. A tall, strong lady, someone who could wear saris like Nayantara's characters did in the movies. I thought of jute silk saris as I cooked rice and curry. I added more turmeric than was needed in the coconut paste. I decided to fry some fish when it was time to eat.

After finishing my work, I sat down under the fan with my phone. In a video shared on our cousins' WhatsApp group, a swami said Muslim men had greater sexual appetite because they ate beef. Upon this, a lady queried in the group whether women who ate beef also had greater sexual appetites. 'If so, we wouldn't need to look up at the dirt on the fan while we were at it.' All the women in the group roared with laughter.

As the conversation flowed towards triple talaq and polygamy, one of the cousins appeared with a post: 'Semen that enters a woman's womb will be washed out only after three menstrual cycles.' He said this was the scientific basis for the Islamic law that women could get remarried only after observing *iddah* for four months and ten days after her husband's demise. Hearing such absurdities, a doctor in the group lost her temper. But the man was reluctant to believe her. He asked, 'What is the relevance of *iddah* then?'

'Even if a woman despised her husband, she wouldn't rush into another marriage soon after his death,' I said. 'And being locked up in a room alone while she was going through a difficult time would just add to her trauma.'

We finished off the man when he said, 'You are a pseudo-intellectual!'

We laughed once more while telling the cousin who had come from the UAE for a two-month-long vacation that if she got pregnant when her hubby was not with her she could claim his semen had been floating inside her for four months.

Mohini had no such fears. She slept with many men every day. But it all changed the day she appeared before her father. This is the twist.

The phone rang, with its usual habit of interrupting

my thoughts. It was Neema. She wanted me to come with her to the hospital. Her legs were aching. The doctor had advised her not to travel.

Every time the auto jumped over a pothole, I held my abdomen as if I were the one who was pregnant. As we joined the long queue in front of the gynaecologist's consulting room, Neema said, 'Let's tell the doctor we are a lesbian couple.' Looking around at the people, she then said, 'This place is filled with *your* people. They come to see a doctor as if they are attending a wedding, and they feast inside the hospital.'

There were two consulting rooms ahead of us. The names on the boards announced the religion of the doctors – one Muslim, one Hindu. People entered the rooms as their names were called out. After a while, Neema said, 'All the patients going into that room are *your* people. I have heard that your people only consult a Muslim doctor.' I didn't ask her why no Hindus were walking into that room. If they had a heart attack, they would surely forget their religion and caste and rush to the nearest doctor clutching at their chests, I thought.

Should I include a scene where the doctor had a heart attack? He was going through difficult times. But he was also seeking revenge in novel ways without shedding a tear. His wife too was stoic as she pointed out to the police that her daughter's nipple was out of place and was now in her navel. Manu flew into a rage saying the police were insensitive to show the mutilated body of the girl to her mother. He was on the verge of collapse when he took Veni's mother home, who said, 'Ask the doctor to return from Delhi immediately. He is a great surgeon. Everything must be put back in its right place. I will tell him where each part has to be placed. A mother knows her daughter better than the father.' She went upstairs to change her sari and shut the door, only to change her life into death.

Who should be the music director? Vishal Bhardwaj would rock. I decided to narrate the story to the gang. If they liked it, I had nothing to fear.

I announced on the WhatsApp group, 'I'm writing a story.'

Everyone was excited. It had been a long time since I had written one. 'Shreddies' came up with the question, 'Is it erotica?'

We were all twisted branches that had sprung out from the same root. We called each other only by nicknames. The one who peeped at women in a Dubai swimming pool was 'Peeping Tom', 'Peeps' for short; the married man who still thought about his lover was 'Rooster'. The women of APC, the Anti-Panty Committee, hated wearing bra and panties. We would need to create a new dictionary if I explained all the names. When I narrated the story, 'Mongoose' objected, 'Why do you always write about rape?'

'Spy' and 'Cuckoo' chimed in with their criticism too.

'Isn't there any other topic to write about? Men have problems too. They are also sexually exploited.'

'Angry bird' responded, 'Whether it's men or women at the receiving end, it's always men who exploit.'

As the males chorused their objections, I posted another question: 'Tell me about a recent incident that has troubled you.'

When 'Shreddies' said, 'I am disturbed by a porn clip I couldn't get hold of,' I said, 'Buzz off, bugger.'

He replied, 'Don't get angry. Continue with your story.'

'This is not my story so I shouldn't write it,' I said.

'I know the climax. The surgeon turned the male rapist into a female, Mohini.'

'You aren't just a mere monkey, but Hanuman himself!'

'Don't play with Hanuman. If you do so, your home will turn into a Hanuman temple.'

'Don't come this way or else they will turn you into the monkey deity.'

'Such a poor joke! I'm going to office. Do you know what time it is?'

'Oh, I just remembered I have to link my Aadhaar card to my bank account.'

'What else is left to link?' he asked.

'Underwear,' I snubbed him and switched off my internet.

The bus was quite empty when I got on, so I got a seat. I let my hair fly as the driver picked up speed. When the bus went down a slope, the driver braked suddenly. I hit my head against the back of the seat in front of me. Nobody heard the curses I muttered under my breath in the commotion. There had been a collision between a lorry coming from the opposite direction and a car that had overtaken us. Some passengers got down to see the accident. I felt my legs tremble. When I heard someone say two children aged two and five had died on the spot, I felt a sour liquid rise up in my mouth.

As I wondered how I could erase the memory of this journey from my mind, I heard all seven had died.

'They are not *our people*.'

Was it a secret whisper? Had someone said this? Or had I imagined it after hitting my head against the seat?

The sour taste in my mouth turned bitter.

THE BOOK RELEASE

'My father was a Malayalam teacher.'

The sub-inspector looked at the paper on his table once again.

'Did you write this?'

'I wanted to be a writer.'

As she recited the Malayalam alphabet like a lullaby, mispronouncing most of it, she felt the first slap.

Aghast, the first grader looked at her father. She could feel a trickle of pee wetting her panties.

The tone of my father's voice had embedded the letters in the crevices of my brain. I was remembering the grammar lessons when I noticed the SI was carefully looking at me.

'Who else is at home?'

'Amma.'

'Kummanam to Meet the Central Team'

'Curbing Public Opinion is the Sangh Parivar's fascist style of operation: Chief Minister'

'People in fear, CM must give up Home Ministry: Opposition leader'

I looked at the newspaper. The front page carried photos of all five of them. The SI's eyes, which followed my glance, clearly asked the question, 'Why?'

I loved words. I would write down whatever caught my fancy in notebooks. My father read out the poem I had written in my notebook. He read each word aloud. I was too old to wet myself. Then he asked, 'What is the meaning of *'Kettipidichaalingnam'*?*

He told me go to the pillar and put my arms around it. He enunciated carefully – *'kettipidichu'* first, then *'aalinganam'* – and said it twice to prove my mistake. I felt the cane cut into my flesh as I hugged the pillar, like a fish being slit open before being marinated.

'She's just a child,' my mother whispered from behind the door.

'When will I scold her then? When she reaches your age?'

That poetic adventure turned into an elegy for me. The people who arrived at my table that day were Hemingway,

---

* The two words, kettipidichu and aalinganam have the same meaning – 'to hug'.

Shaw and Basheer – writers who remind us that verbal jugglery was not what made them immortal.

I read till words stung my eyes. Each time the malady of writing recurred, the cane rose higher into the air. I didn't want to expose the cartography of my mistakes on my legs, so I started wearing long skirts to high school as Muslim girls did. By then, my table was filled with books on literary criticism. My writing suffered as the writer knew too much.

The easiest task was to capture the prince of romance. I got hold of his phone number and sent him messages constantly as if I were an ardent admirer. From the second day onwards, honeyed words flowed in the form of 'good night, my love' and red hearts.

I felt nauseated as I typed grammatically incorrect sentences in 'Manglish' – a combination of Malayalam and English – that said I adored his works and wanted to kiss his fingers and lay my head on his chest. I thought of Raj Malhotra, my NIT classmate, and of the days I had stood next to him in the laboratory, inhaling his scent, touching him as if by accident. The nights I spent thinking about him. I used to imagine him writing on my cheek with his beard and long to touch his soft cheeks on the days he shaved. I thought of the fever inside me. How many letters had I written to him in my imagination? What worried me more than my parents finding out about my romance with Raj was whether my father would discover the errors of language in the letters. As I didn't know Hindi, I could only write in Malayalam. He was the love I never spoke about as I feared that my father would collapse to the ground if he learnt I was in love with a man who didn't know Malayalam. If only I had sent him a message such as the one I sent now:

'Tomorrow, on Vishu, I will come to meet you!'

'But tomorrow isn't Vishu.'

'It is, because the laburnums will bloom when we meet.'

If my father overheard this conversation, he would put a wreath of laburnum over my body.

'My beautiful baby!'

'Well, you have to give me a gift on Vishu. Wear your blue shirt and dhoti. Don't put on any underwear.'

I would go to his house in a mundu and a veshti, with jasmine flowers in my hair and a red bindi on my forehead. Blending adoration, coyness and enthusiasm, I performed the Mohiniyattam dance with my eyes. As I tied his hands to the chair and asked him not to be naughty, he became hard and his dhoti rose like a tent. My work was easy after that. His eagerness lay on the floor like a black bug. I collected his books and made a bonfire out of them. Those who crucified my favourite poet Kamala Das for her writing, one who wrote beautiful lines like, 'My love is like wild honey; many springs have been mixed in it,' made him the prince of love. Bullshit! I smiled at him as he sat numb, watching his blood gush out of his nether region. It was only after I got into the auto that I realized I hadn't told him why I killed him.

'Ayyo! This book was written by our sir!'

The SI let out a gasp when I put the book on the table. I felt he would jump up and salute.

'Have you read it?'

'Where do I have the time to read? But I bought a copy the day it was released.'

'I was there too. The media had widely publicized the release.'

He stared at me.

A female police officer came in to meet the SI. I named her 'Saramma'. Her expression, when she saw the book on the table, resembled the emoticon that showed disdain. I was sure she had read the book. I liked her. But why do we call a slightly plump and dark woman 'Saramma'? Let her be a 'Nandana' or an 'Ammu'. 'Ammu Police' had a nice ring to it. I ignored the badge on her chest with her name engraved on it. 'Ammu Police' had a nice bum. If the glances that pierced it could leave marks, her bum would resemble my legs.

I had to travel a long way to get to the writer's house. I thought I would meet him and return. The rest could be decided later. But when I got there, he was alone. He told me everyone else had gone to watch Theyyam (but wasn't Theyyam conducted at night?). I told him that I was a journalist who had come for an interview. As I had read most of his books, it was easy to ask questions.

'Have you really read Márquez?'

He frowned when I asked him this question, trying to learn if it held a deeper meaning.

'At a recent book release, I heard you praising a mediocre book to the skies. That can be forgiven. But you compared the writer to Márquez, you said Malayalam literature had not seen such an intensely romantic novel before, and that all of us were eagerly awaiting his next book. I have to kill you for speaking such filth.'

Contrary to my expectations, he didn't look shocked at all. He ran his fingers through his fluffy white hair and sat down, as if he were lost in thought, before beginning to speak:

'There was a time when the desire to write drove me

mad. At times, I waited for days for the right word to occur to me. I discarded much of what I wrote because I wasn't satisfied with it. But fame has its own drawbacks. You will have to put yourself in difficult situations. You may have to do things that make you despise yourself – writing prefaces, book releases and so on. I felt it would have been better to repair umbrellas for a living – at least people would have benefitted.'

It was he who put his hand on my forehead and handed me the pillow as he lay on the bed. I felt sad when I pressed the pillow on his face.

'This is the first time I am seeing a police station. I had only seen it in movies till now.'

'Where are you studying? Do you have an ID card?'

As I handed over my ID card, I thought it must be some formality.

The SI called Ammu Police and gave her the card. Ammu sashayed away.

'Do you want coffee?'

'Your superior, the writer, offered me coffee too when I visited him.'

'Did you go there as well?'

'Yes, and I told him that he wrote trash.'

'Did you say that?'

'I am not afraid of anyone. Do you know what I did after reading his book? I bought several romantic novels and sent them to him. I had to spend a lot of money. It's not that Achan's cupboard didn't have such stuff, but if he found a book missing, I would be killed. *Anna Karenina*, *Love in the Time of Cholera*, *Days of Love*, and *Dona Flor and Her Two Husbands* – have you read it? It's an excellent book. Do you know how much I cried after reading *Wuthering Heights*? Cathy and Heathcliff! Finally, I sent him Rafeeq Ahmed's poem, "As death approaches":

The last breath I draw
must carry your scent.

'Can people love so much? He must have been deeply in love.'

'How did you kill Sir?'

When he asked me that question, I was humming the rest of the poem in my mind. I do not like to be disturbed when I am thinking. But I couldn't say that to police officers. I noticed a smile hiding behind his moustache. All subordinates resent their superiors.

'Why should I tell you everything? It is up to you to find out. If the courtroom scenes are left out, it would be a dull novel.'

'Novel?'

'I have decided to write a novel based on my experiences

inside jail: a woman's narrative. I am sure it would be a bestseller. I've even decided on the dedication:

To,

My Father

My body was violated every time he caned me. He trespassed on my body. He might not have realized that it was my mind that was wounded.

'The cane is a phallic symbol.'

I don't think he understood what I said. There was no sense of comprehension on his face. He had to answer a few calls, so he asked me to leave after that. He said I would be called in after they completed the inquiries. I was furious. I shouted at them. I can't remember what I said. But they wanted me to go home after I had confessed to killing five people.

'You are eager to torture innocent people to death in the lock-up. I will call the media here and tell them everything.'

That is all I recollect. By then, Ammu Police made me sit and tried to calm me down. After making a number of phone calls, the SI came up to me.

'Come, we have to go.'

'To jail?'

'We need to complete certain formalities before that. We have to meet higher officials.'

I thought that was a good idea. Everything would happen quickly. I struck up a conversation with Ammu Police in the jeep.

'I am saying this to you because I like you. You read a lot, so you will understand. It was when I killed the painter that I felt really sad. He was my friend, and he had given me books to read. But I couldn't bear it when he compared that trashy writer to Calvino. If I had a gun, I would have finished him on the spot. Do you know what he said when I asked him about it? He said he was being sarcastic! But even senior writers didn't catch on.'

I wanted to tell him he should have gauged the intellectual abilities of his listeners before using sarcasm, but I decided not to say this over the phone and went to meet him.

He was in his garden, watering the plants he had planted himself. He was happy to see me and took me to his library. He asked if I wanted jaggery coffee (actually, he just said coffee, but I am trying to exoticize our meeting). With great pride he showed me a copy of Mário de Andrade's *Macunaíma* for which he had paid ₹8,000. I wondered for a moment whether I should let him complete the book. No, he would do the art for the Inspector General's next book too, then claim the writer was like Mario Vargas Llosa.

'What is your favourite colour?'

'Green.'

He looked at me quizzically.

I wondered whether to kill him by holding his head down in a bucket of water mixed with green paint. But I hung him to death on the vines of the white gourd. His legs touched the ground.

Let his feet sprout into roots.

The jeep stopped in front of a building. But it didn't look like a police station. Ammu Police said it was a *Janamaitri*, a 'people-friendly' police station.

As I walked inside, I remember thinking the man with the salt-and-pepper hair was quite good-looking.

'Who is this? Is he a doctor?'

I looked at his nameplate resting on the table. It must have been a psychological move to test me.

'So, how were the murders committed?'

'I have told the SI everything in detail. I told Ammu Police about one of the murders too.

'To be honest, I grew bored after the first two murders. I thought of letting the woman writer who had come for the book release live. But the speech she made while clutching the mike… as if hungry children had suddenly seen food! The feminist in me boiled with anger and asked me how I could not include at least one woman among my victims. But she wasn't fit to be my prey. I even wondered whether I should give her more publicity by killing her. Don't you think she is overrated? She is famous only because she belongs to the minority.'

'Does religion work in such matters too?'

I laughed. 'This is the best joke anyone has cracked in Kerala.'

I liked the way he spoke, looking into my eyes. As we talked, Ammu Police came in and spoke to him.

'Please go to the next room. You can rest there.'

The conversation was rudely interrupted. I wanted coffee. I would ask Ammu Police to get me one.

'Don't worry. She is a sensitive girl. She is also a good reader,' the doctor told the bewildered father. 'As she is studying engineering, her studies must be putting a lot of pressure on her. We will begin medication.'

Though he had given the same advice to many people, this was the first time he said, 'Don't let her attend any book releases.'

As my father walked away like words in a jumbled sentence, the doctor called him back. He handed over a book the daughter had left on his table to the father. 'Don't let her read such books.'

RECOGNITION

There are certain faces one remembers only in specific contexts. Perhaps that was why Raghavan and Catherine didn't recognize each other at the airport.

A dispute regarding the sharing of the prize money at the 1998 Nehru Trophy Boat Race had led to the establishment of the Victory Boat Club. The Kumarakom Thekkekara residents who broke away from the Union Boat Club decided they would have their own boat club from thereon. Union Boat Club would come to be known as 'UBC', while the Thekkekara residents decided to call theirs 'VBC'.

Raghavan, the boatman who belonged to Thekkekara, was the third oarsman at UBC. But in the 1999 Nehru Trophy Boat Race, held after the split, he was the first oarsman of the *Payippad Chundan* boat which belonged to VBC. During the twenty days of practice, Raghavan headed the oarsmen and threw his oar into the water first.

He had lost his father when he was seventeen, and had started taking out his father's boat to ferry travellers and save his mother and sister from hunger. His house was near the river, so one could take the boat out even at night in case of emergencies. This was also one of the reasons why Raghavan and his father got their contract to ferry the boat renewed each year. For twenty years, he worked with diligence, never making his passengers wait for long. Each time he took his boat out, he would skim his fingers through the river and splash some water on his face to refresh himself. He knew the water's smell and taste was changing.

Once, as he ferried his old classmate Jayadevan, a Malayalam teacher in Thekkekara, back from work, he told him about the changes in the river. His old classmate, who had turned into a stereotypical Malayalam teacher, stroked his beard and said, 'Water is the truth that runs all over the earth's surface.'

In August, the month set aside for the boat race, Raghavan decided to entrust his boat to his neighbour Rameshan to practise for the race. This was not just a race for them; it was a ritual. Apart from the physical training, Raghavan also had to prepare his mind to compete in the race. An oarsman enters the race as a soldier enters the battlefield. For the people of Kuttanad, rowing a boat was once part of their daily lives. Now, Raghavan's son wouldn't even touch an oar for fun.

Raghavan had learnt several lessons as a child: You should be barefoot when you get onto the boat. You should pray to the gods and your gurus. You have to abstain from liquor, meat and sex. The first oarsman should get into the boat first, then the first rower. The rowers have to sit according to their body weight. All of this begins from the training period itself. Continuous practice sessions were held so that the crew could maintain the tempo and row with the same vigour from start to finish.

Raghavan still got goosebumps when he recollected the first time he had competed in a race. He was more excited than when he had touched Shanthamma for the first time. He felt like a pilgrim who climbs the Sabari Hills barefoot after fasting for 41 days, and when they arrive at the sanctum sanctorum, they feel a wave of sheer excitement run through their body that eventually comes out as a prayer – 'Swamiye sharanam' – even as their legs falter. It was more intense than the ecstasy when he rowed through Shanthamma's polished black skin.

Raghavan's life did not leave much room for God or women. He didn't even sprout beliefs as his friends did during exams. It wasn't just because his father was a blazing communist, but also because he had realized that God had limited powers in the matter of exams. He went to Sabarimala because his mother had prayed he would do so if his sister recovered from a serious illness. As it concerned his sister, Raghavan did not compromise on his prayer or his abstinence. Once his sister recovered completely, he decided to give Ayyappan some space in his mind. Ayyappan could chat with Marx, who already lived inside. When Raghavan picked up the oar after his father's death, the realization that he was ferrying the dreams of his passengers gave strength to his thin adolescent hands.

Years went by as he ferried passengers from one side of the river to the other and back again. Nothing spectacular happened in his life. He had two children. His mother grew old and stopped going out of their house. When his neighbour Sivaraman's daughter got admission in a nursing college, they didn't let her join for fear that she would fall in love with a Muslim boy and convert to Islam. When elections drew near, groups of people, including women, went to houses telling them not to vote for Christian candidates. Life continued as usual after that wave of fundamentalism passed. It maintained the same rhythm till the next boat race drew near.

Something quite unexpected happened in Raghavan's life this year, though. They were celebrating their victory in a toddy shop when Thekkumpurath Jose ettan's son Anto arrived with two foreigners. Raghavan drank only on festive occasions. Anto translated the mumbo jumbo of the foreigners to him. When he heard Anto, Raghavan wondered whether he had lost his senses even before he had started drinking. They wanted him to row a boat in a competition held somewhere else! *These foreigners know nothing about what is to be done. They think rowing is easy. But how can one blame them? Even in Kerala we have started hiring itinerant labourers from other states to row in competitions.* Muttering all this to himself, Raghavan left the toddy shop.

Anto came home the next morning and started his prattle. 'You tell him, Shanthedathi! He is wasting his time here, earning a pittance. This is such a good offer. They will buy the tickets and arrange for his stay. They will also pay him well. If he wins, spectators will shower him with gifts. This Dragon Festival is a great celebration there. They were impressed by his rowing skills and that is why they came to him without approaching anyone else. Yet he is saying the boat race here is a ritual and all that shit.'

Raghavan didn't say anything as he thought Anto would be getting a commission. His head was also a bit woozy from yesterday's liquor. He hadn't been able to shit that morning and had asked his wife for tea. Shantha had been about to give him an earful when Anto arrived. By the time Anto left, two teams had formed in his house, and Raghavan was the sole member of his team. It was that moment which decided Raghavan's journey.

Raghavan landed in Singapore, his ears buzzing because of the difference in air pressures. He thought he was in a dream, but one that was a bit too bright. The roads were fit to eat from. Buildings here couldn't be measured by the eyes. He immediately decided it was a magical place. He was relieved a Malayali had come to fetch him. James explained everything to Raghavan. A lift inside the building went up like a rocket. They reached a room and a card opened the door. As he stood in the cold room, he felt a sting in his eyes as he remembered his boat and the coldness of the river water. James left saying, 'Rest now. We will go out later.'

When he reached the race venue, his eyes popped out. The boat looked like an eggshell, and the people around were so fair even their eyes seemed white. There were women rowers as well! But when he grew familiar with his surroundings, he felt he could manage the competition. Although they didn't know his language, they were disciplined people and grasped things quickly. They faithfully followed his instructions and treated him with great respect, perhaps because they were not divided by caste. He remembered the caste name by which he was addressed in school: 'Chovvan'. The practice sessions were held conscientiously, and the race was breathtaking. As his boat overtook the competitors', Raghavan stood with his head held high, comforted by the thought that he had not let down the people who had trusted him.

The organizers held a party at an expensive restaurant that night. Thankfully the menu had none of the insects and reptiles that he had seen being sold on the pavement when they had taken him sightseeing. James brought him a tall crystal glass filled with liquor. He said, 'This is your day! Enjoy,' before walking away. His glass remained topped-up, along with handshakes and pats on the back. Raghavan did not even realize a pair of red lips began dragging him away. Leaving her to row, he lay back like a boat.

It started at a slow rhythmic pace, Raghavan saw the church on the right and the boat jetty on the left. He thought he could hear a long whistle. He sat up and rowed fiercely. The leap of victory had begun. He knew if they could lunge forward at the point near the church, they would win. He heard the applause as they reached the finishing point.

Between the gasps and the moans, Catherine asked him, 'Are you from Kuttanad?'

The journey to Kerala and the rhythm of the boat race flashed in her half-shut eyes.

UPSIDE DOWN

What did the doctor say?

Game over.

Don't joke. Tell me what the doctor said?

I'm going to die soon. You better round up your old girlfriends. The one who said she will come in an Audi, or the one who said she thinks of you while she sleeps with her husband. Or the one you taught how to wear a sari. Who will you call? Maybe find a new one – a dusky beauty.

This is a cliché. You are overdoing it. It's boring.

Now I am a bore to you!

....

Hey, did I annoy you?

Tell me what the doctor said?

The doctor asked me if I could reduce my intelligence.

Shut up! Arrogant wretch.

I have lost my balance. The world seems upside down. America is now at the bottom.

You are crazy!

I had a dream. Do you want to hear about it?

Tell me.

I am bald, and a woman is rubbing glue all over my head to stick a wig on it. But wouldn't it hurt when I took it off? I thought of you peeling it off my head. Then I said, 'I don't want this wig. I want to get off the bus with my bald head and walk past the group of boys who used to wait for me.'

To tell you the truth, you have watched too many chick-lit movies. Bald head! My foot!

Look! A cat is watching me. It's just staring at me.

Cats are always half-asleep, as if lost in the memories of their past births when they were tigers.

Do you think I was a tiger in my previous life?

Maybe, and you may have been cursed to behave like a cat in this birth too.

Yes, I think so too.

Look into the mirror. Look as if you aren't you.

Do you want to add to my madness?

My mad beauty.

I don't want dinner. I am flattered!

Why this upside-down emoticon?

Isn't the earth spinning?

It must be raining somewhere, right?

I long to watch rain – proper torrential rain.

We have the summer of a century blazing outside.

We will have to make it rain inside.

Rains. Deaths. Shall we freeze the twilight too?

Yes.

Have you seen the sun glisten on the river at twilight?

The sun, yes, but not the river.

The river will be in your memory.

Is it the earth that is spinning, or my head?

Your head for sure. The earth must be staring at your head.

Ohhh!

What are you doing?

Reading.

Whom?

Someone flaunting his caste.

That is the vestige of a bygone era.

That caste pride is growing.

Yes. I don't read anything that has a caste attached to it.

I am losing my balance.

Did you get it back?

No.

What will you do? Have you discovered the world revolves around you?

It is a nice feeling.

Is it a story that's making your head spin?

I hadn't thought of that. Yes, I am sure it is such a story. I have heard stories have a habit of doing this.

I see everything upside down.

Magical realism?

Only magic.

Wow!

Shall I tell you another dream? One that I just saw.

Yes.

I get off the train at Parappanangadi, the place where I was born. The place has changed. When I reach my ancestral house, I see a newly built house in its place. I don't go in. I walk ahead, along a narrow path, and reach a cave. The cave Priya and I had entered. (There is no such place. But narrow paths and caves recur in my dreams.) I think I should go inside. I walk a long way and reach a place filled with greenery. There is a railway station here. A few people are sitting as if to warm themselves in the sun. I cross the railway track and walk on. There are fields on either side. Not fields really, but meadows, like you see in an English countryside. An expanse of green with a silk ribbon of a path in the middle. I reach a crossing. There are some trains there. I cut across the railway lines.

Then?

Then you woke me up. I tried to cling to the edges of

my dream. But I was disturbed, as if a journey had been interrupted. The train blocked my view and I couldn't see where I went.

Shall we consult another doctor?

No way. I want to walk away with the rain.

Rain can preserve lost memories in its depths.

There are rains we don't see, like how we don't see moments that are fleeting.

How was the black tea? I made it in my previous birth.

It had an atavistic taste. Like when we turn back time, like a hot rain that hid in a memory of tea gardens.

Shall I hide you within the story?

Don't tell anyone.

It is a secret. Only you know where you are hidden.

In the depths of the well.

Hiding is a joy, as is being discovered.

The well, where disembodied joys meet.

It is cold there.

Just touch the lips of the wind.

Why are you laughing?

I remembered your lips.

I like it when you are mad. It is then that you love me most.

Shall I leave now? Don't go off with anyone else.

Oh, I forgot to ask you.

Yes?

When I die, will you bring me a wreath of violets?

Fuck off.

Thank you.

MY NOTEBOOK

I'm bruised and burning. My arms and legs ache. The thing he asked me to hold is slimy. I thought of the first pencil I owned. My uncle held my hand and took me to school for the first time. And I carried the pencil with me. Both the pencil and the school were yellow in colour. Do you know? My first pencil was yellow with black stripes all over it. I named it 'Yellow Zebra'. The rabbit-shaped eraser on top of the pencil was pink and looked like a ripe *jamun*. It smelled like the baby at home, and also of candy. Once I bit into it, unable to control my greed. A bit of the eraser rebelled against me for pushing it into the dark hole of my belly. When it threatened to erase my belly, I was scared.

Ah! This man will cut me in two. I shut my eyes tight and think of writing a letter to Ammi and Appa.

Why did they give me away to a stranger? Why did they send me to a strange house? I have an exam tomorrow.

My classmates must be staying up late to study. Our class teacher had warned us that anyone who didn't manage a first class would not move to the eighth grade. I'm scared of Maths, but I like Malayalam and English, especially the stories and the poems. I like writing my thoughts down in my notebook too. But Appa took away my notebook. He said girls needn't learn how to read and write. They must recite the Quran and do housework – that's all they are meant to do.

Is he pumping air? Chhotu had a bicycle and a pump. I used to fill his tyres with air. He was overjoyed when I drew a picture of his cycle in my notebook.

I want to sleep. I want to curl up on my grandmother's lap as I often did. She would run her fingers through my hair and start telling me stories. Lying in her lap, I could see the palace under the sea and the world beyond the seven skies. But one morning, she didn't wake up. A lot of people came home that day. A few of them took her to the bathroom outside to bathe her. They wrapped her in a white cloth patterned with henna. She looked like a tea cake wrapped in white paper, with the paper twisted at both ends. I loved to eat that cake when I got back from school. She smelled of *pandan* flowers at all times. She always had the flowers in her trunk. My notebooks carried her fragrance, their pages as smooth as her love.

Why is this man panting like a dog? I hate dogs. Ammi has told me I would have to bathe seven times if I touched a dog. 'Ammi, I'm dirty.'

I will take a dip in the well. I will climb down the deep well to see the palace beneath. Do not call me back.

GREEN AND VIOLET STARS

Stars are the souls of memories. My sky is filled with stars – of dreams, desires and thoughts. It's a sky full of stars that are always out of my reach. When you fall ill, the world turns dark. Perhaps the whole world seems drowsy because I didn't open my eyes. In the evenings, my mind fills itself with unknown sorrows. As it is I am tired because of the fever. I can't eat anything. If my stomach had a zipper, I would open it and stuff it with food.

He asks me, 'Didn't you just have Horlicks and two sweet limes?' A friend pipes up, 'Usually people grow pale when they get fever, but with her, you can't tell the difference.' (I wonder who began calling me 'ghost'.) The mustard seed caught between his front teeth disturbs me. But I cannot tell him about it.

I love travelling alone. My thoughts flow freely then. I watch my fellow travellers. Some are quite like life itself.

They barge in and establish a friendship with you, and within minutes, they behave as if they have known you forever. Suddenly, they leave, when the bus arrives at their destination.

The fragrance that flowed from the woman who sat next to me on the bus took me back to Arifa's garden filled with violets. Arifa was my classmate in 3B. I have not seen such flowers since then, nor have I met Arifa after leaving school. Why is the ticket examiner staring at me? Do I have horns? Luckily, he can't see my tail. Shall I write a note to the guy waiting by the roadside?

Nityakalyani, who called me to complain that I never wrote to her, wanted to know what had kept me too busy to write. I told her I had turned the house upside down and was now washing the dirt off the foundation.

The man with the beard has a nice smile. But I couldn't understand what he was saying. I wish I had a small cushion to rest my hand. My elbow hurts, but I rested my face on it, carrying on with my daydream. As the class went on, a wide-eyed girl sent me a note, 'I love you so much.' When a boy saw it, he said, 'Whew! It's safe to walk with you. I was worried.'

I couldn't even see the toenails of the man who said women were the cause of all problems. Now he is head over heels in love. When he called me last evening, he said, 'Love is like diabetes – it just shoots up.'

'What are you scribbling?' The bearded teacher was right in front of me.

'Sir, my diary is in tatters and I forgot to write down the page numbers.'

I.D.

He and I were close to the sky. People and vehicles around us grew smaller and smaller. This must be how God sees us: small bodies filled with envy, malice, love, lust, sorrow and pride, all incessantly moving in different directions. It was nice to be God for a while.

He threw away my white dress saying I didn't need a cover when I was with him. Twilight brimmed over.

'Your cheeks turn red at times.'

He searched for the red in my cheeks. 'Then your left leg begins twitching, and you cover your eyes with your hand and smile, enveloped by shyness.'

'Pathu, I live in those moments.'

Poetry thickened in his eyes:

Body of my woman, I will
Persist in your grace,
My thirst, boundless desire,

My shifting road
Dark riverbed where
Eternal thirst flows
And weariness follows and
The eternal ache.

I wanted to tell him about the man who told me he would wait till he became old to kiss the black mole on my cheek. No, I wouldn't live till then. I'm rubbing the lifeline on my palm to erase it. Even though the skin came off, the line didn't go anywhere.

Does my palm, which I had folded into a fist when I entered this world, contain within it the pages of my life? There are so many lines! Did my mother's love for her child diminish when I sucked my thumb and refused her breast milk? There was no other reason why I turned out to be so headstrong.

When I was a child, a friend used to ask me to think of something I loved. She told me she knew a mantra that would make my hands smell of whatever I thought about. I have smelled biscuits, pencils, pens, paints, letters, trains, books, chalk pieces, curries, dewdrops on flowers, clothes, sand, rain and the green of the leaves. My palms have carried a variety of fragrances. And now, the smell of his thick, dark, curly hair. I have to save the smell of it in my palm till we meet again.

I had not met Tanvi, or Tanu, for a while now. Romance

had gone to her head and she wandered aimlessly. There she was now, looking dishevelled.

'What has happened to you? Did you both fight?' She is an artist. Colours, fragrances and beauty make up her world.

Her phone rang. It was Hemanth. She did not answer.

'Did you fight?' I joked.

'Paru, we got some time together – alone. We were kissing passionately, when suddenly he burped. I could smell the chutney he had eaten for breakfast. I came away.'

That's Tanu, the woman with a world-renowned nose.

Terrified of the dark evenings when her father who reeked of liquor turned up, and scared of the smells, she had begun to crunch crisps. Each time she was insecure, she would start eating. She would finger the folds on her belly and say, 'Like tyres heaped together.'

'You will have to display a notice board on your first night – "Humps ahead. Go slow",' Nikitha quipped. She laughed at her own joke, that girl with the unruly hair. Trying to cheer up Tanu, I said, 'Look, let us make her the hero in our new-gen movie. Curly hair, an oversized pair of spectacles, a side profile with a large coffee mug in her hand and soft music playing in the background.'

With mischief dancing in her eyes, Nikitha said, 'Paru, the *Kamasutra* says a woman who looks out of a window isn't satisfied with her sexual life.'

'Girl, first try and pass the exams you flunked last year.

Clear your back papers instead of acting smart with me!'

This world, this room in the hostel made me feel secure. I lived here as their Paru and his Pathu.

'Tanu, aren't you coming to class? It's been so many days since you attended one. Come, let's see what they have in the mess today.' I forced her.

'It will be the usual. Idlis you can use as a stone to throw at someone, or puttu that will get stuck in your throat, or bread that has attained salvation inside the fridge. I'm eating out.'

Being with Nikitha was like witnessing the dawn of spring. She was vivacious. Her eyes, her cheeks, her unruly hair – even the air around her seemed to be filled with energy. Her brightly coloured clothes, her bangles that seemed to jingle and chatter as much as she did, her glittering nose ring – everything seemed to be bursting with life.

Research scholars were given single rooms in the hostel. As Nikitha had low marks, it had taken her a while to get admission into a degree course at the college. By then, the hostel was full, and she was asked to stay in my room temporarily. I tried with all my might to resist this intrusion into my private space. But Nikitha forced her way in and made me her Paru. At times, she even turned me into her older sister, calling me 'Paru chechi'. Tanu would also drop in at times to chat.

I went out saying I had to go to the library to write a

paper for a conference. I called out, 'Tanu, lock the door when you leave.'

Tanu was lying on the bed. It was no use talking to her when she had these mood swings. She wouldn't stir. When she came out of it, she would say, 'The vehicle was switched off, so it took a while to get it moving.'

It was late when I returned. Nikitha and Tanu were celebrating. The table was overflowing with packages. I didn't like to bring food inside the room and they knew it well. But Nikitha began with a winning smile, 'Paru, Tanu just sold a painting and she is giving us a treat. Don't worry, we will clean up. Come, let's party.'

When I came out after a bath, they had laid the table. Nikitha began to sing and dance.

'I am going abroad. I don't want to study commerce anymore. I want to study art. Paris, here I come!' Tanu announced, hugging Nikitha and twirling her around.

'I am tired of this place. People look at me and say, "This girl is wandering around drawing pictures. Who will give her a steady job?" Behind my back, they snigger and say, "Look how fat she is! Who will want to marry her?"'

'Both of you are missing classes. You act as if your ticket to Paris has already been booked.' I turned into the stern older sister.

'Paru, what is the use of studying?' Nikitha asked, looking at the many voluminous books on my table. 'When girls grow up, they must become teachers. They are waiting for me to complete my graduation to enrol me into a teaching course at some teacher training college. Others want to become nurses and migrate to the US. In between, I will have to meet prospective grooms. Mama said, "There's a good proposal that has come. They are willing to allow you to study more." Who wants their permission? I am thinking of marrying a girl, someone who will take care of me, clean the house, and wash my clothes.'

'What a good idea! Why didn't we think of it before?' Tanu joined Niki.

'Guys, what's actually happening? Nikitha, don't think I haven't noticed Sourav chasing your skirt.'

'Well, thanks to him, my food cravings are taken care of – chocolates, ice-cream… I am not interested in romance. Romance is boring. So many rules: you have to walk with him; you cannot look at anyone else; can't talk to other people; you should only eat what he likes; you must think of him all the time – and remember his first words to you, his first gift, where he touched you first. It's so complicated! If my memory was good enough to remember all of this, I would have gotten into IAS. Haven't I told you what happened when I went for the school tour during my plus-2? My friend Neelima didn't really get to see any sights that day. Nor could she have fun with us. As we swam, her boyfriend's command to her was, "Don't step into the water. Men will be around." She then stood by clutching her phone, watching us. "You should never fall in love when you are a student. You will lose the best part of your life."'

'When should we fall in love then? When we turn into grandmothers?' I touched her dimple.

'Why should one fall in love? I am with Sourav today. Tomorrow, it will be Gaurav. It is better to make friends with girls. Only they can understand us. We can walk around freely without being pestered by prying eyes. We can ogle at good-looking boys and maybe fantasize about them at night.'

'What about marriage? Oh, but you are marrying a docile, well-behaved girl, right?' Tanu laughed.

'My dear Tanu, why would anyone want a love marriage? The love will get over right after the wedding. You start thinking about what to cook for breakfast, you watch him sleep with his mouth open at night, you wash his underclothes. Any woman will start wondering why she left her family to marry this guy.'

I gave a knock on her head and asked, 'And which country will you rule, Nikitha Khrushchev? You don't want to study, you don't want a job, and you don't want to fall in love!'

'Paru, what can a girl desire?' Niki began talking like a

grown-up. The naivety in her eyes faded and the light of determination shone through. 'How much freedom does a girl have? Will she become liberated if she has a job? Can she spend her earnings on what she wants to do? Won't she always be held tight by her home? Won't an ordinary woman's life be spent between home, office, kitchen and her children? No, I want to see the world. I want to travel. I want to know the taste of distant lands. I want to mark the sights I see with a Mark 7D camera. Haven't you read Wim Wenders's book *Once*? I want to do something like that – wander like a modern-day gypsy. I will marry a filthy rich guy. I can't spend my life wondering about what to cook next.'

What does this child know? What is life without love that burns within you? Where will she find the world that you see only when you lay your head on your lover's chest? I pulled out a chair on the veranda and opened a book. It would be a while before their celebrations wound down.

Gift him all,
Gift him what makes you woman, the scent of
Long hair, the musk of sweat between the breasts,
The warm shock of menstrual blood...

Kamala Das's words showered profuse love. The book had grown swollen because I had turned the pages continually. Now its pages didn't just contain her poetry, they also carried the weight of my passion and longing. He and I – we had bought this book together. We have read the same page sitting in different places. We only needed the page number to remember the poems and recite them.

When Niki came to call me, I was sleeping with the book open in my lap. The room had been cleaned up. Stepping over Tanu's leg that jutted out from under the cot where she lay sleeping, I got into bed. Tanu had always said she felt most secure while sleeping under the cot. Switching the light off, Niki came and lay down, her hand draping over me.

'Chechi, why don't you ever go home?' she asked.

'There's no one at home.'

'No one?'

'No one.'

'Our vacations will start soon. Why don't you come home with me?'

'I am going to Hyderabad. I have some reference work to finish.'

Willing her to not ask any more questions, I turned over and shut my eyes.

Just as I had been thinking I hadn't seen him for a while, he came to meet me. Without going to our usual haunts, we delved into the crowd at Coffee House and pulled up two chairs. His eyes wandered and refused to meet mine. The milk in my coffee had curdled before it reached the table.

He began saying something about matching horoscopes… his sister's future… an exchange marriage…

I wanted to laugh. What a clichéd melodrama. I got up and ran my fingers through the curly hair that had fallen on his forehead. 'I will pay for this. Your expenses have risen.'

I walked out, into myself.

I went home that day after a long time. When I left this house, I was confident because he was with me. Now, my mind was blank. Most of my plants had withered away thirsting for water. Amma was never keen on gardening. The first thing Achan and I had planted was a mango tree. I remembered him telling me the tree would yield mangoes only when my children were born. Surprise was writ large on Amma's face when she opened the door.

'Amma, why don't you water these plants?'

'Oh, I didn't know your ladyship was arriving today. You never bothered to find out how I was. You were just eight when your father passed away. From then on, I...'

Oh, melodrama in the second half as well!

'My father died from a heart attack, not because of me. Please live your life for your own sake, Amma, at least from now on. I am going to Delhi next week. I got a job there.'

Though it was a lie, I was entertained by the suffusion

of expressions on my mother's face. It was a sight to store in my memory. She had believed what I told her. During dinner, she asked me about my job and where I would stay. I felt I should tell Tanu and Niki the same story. Research had begun to sound like a farce, a bunch of pages only three or four people would read. Years spent arranging words on a page that wouldn't benefit society or me. I wanted to leave for a place where I would be far away from my relatives' clutches. I needed to go away to a place where I could be of some use.

But you can call it a departure only when there is someone to call you back.

MALU'S WORLD

I am Malu. I wonder who burdened me with such a horrible name. Most movies and TV soaps have a character named Malu. I want a name that belongs to no one but me.

'Malu, what are you up to? It is almost nine.' It was my mother. The power would go out at 9 p.m. You had to eat dinner and wash up before, as if disaster would strike if you didn't eat on time. Is life to be lived like this? Doing things on time, being precise, punctual? I wish I had a fast-forward button so I could end this farce.

But why should I wait? There are so many ways. One could always take pills. Do you know how much time I have spent thinking about how one can get hold of such pills? I don't want to hang myself. I will look ugly when my friends come to see me, with my tongue protruding. Another option was the train. But I never liked trains. They smell of iron. Their colour resembled mud mixed with sweat. The best way was for a snake to bite me. I could then write emotional letters to my dear ones. There would be enough tears to float a mega serial. I grew excited just thinking about it. But when even pictures of snakes scared me, how could I look at one in real life?

Why are you upset, Malu?

What else can I do? I can't cry, because teary women disgust me. When my younger brother picked a fight with me, when my friend threatened to leave me and go away, when my mother glared at me for not entering the kitchen – what could I do? My head would start aching. It must be a tumour. I would visualize a hospital scene. My days were numbered; people who loved me would surround me. Should I tonsure my head? (My hair fell so much anyway that I would grow bald soon.)

I wish there was a song everybody sang, like in the movies, and before the song ended, my head would tilt to one side in death.

Oh, Malu, such a clichéd scene. Don't you have anything new? Why can't you help your mother instead of thinking about such foolish things?

Cooking was boring. So much time was wasted on wondering about what to make for lunch, about puttu and kadala or idli and sambar. One should put their feet up on the table, look at the sky and dream. I could float on a soft cloud. I could move with the wind. I could go to Antarctica and eat a piece of ice that had been sprinkled with sugar on a stick. Perhaps not. I would then catch cold, my voice would become squeaky, and I wouldn't be able to sing with Lucky Ali. Maybe I could pray for a magic wand – one that would solve all my problems, including cooking. Amma's complaints about not having a maid would stop. Well, if we could swallow food tablets, all our problems would be over – imagine, three idli tablets and one for sambhar!

You shouldn't be so selfish, Malu. What did you do to your mother yesterday?

Well, she got angry and cursed me. She even asked me to go die. But what did I do? The clothes on the washing line were uneven, so I lit a candle to burn the edges of the clothes to make them all equal in length. I didn't imagine it would catch fire and go up in a blaze. On the way to school, I called Amma from a phone booth. I changed my voice and asked, 'Is this Malu's house?'

'Yes.'

'Which hospital has she been admitted to?'

'Hospital? She has gone to school.'

'So you don't know about the accident?'

I then cut the call.

I could imagine the drama after the call. I got home later than usual. Amma ran and hugged me, her face swollen with all the crying. She kissed me on my forehead. I pretended to be ignorant.

Amma said, 'I wonder who called me. I hope his head is struck by lightning.'

God! Will I have to walk around wearing my father's helmet?

Look, Malu, this isn't right. Don't you know how much everyone loves you?

How do we know how much we love someone? Will we see them in a double role in our dreams?

This is your problem, Malu – your wanton thoughts. Make a funeral pyre in your mind and burn down such thoughts.

But where is my mind? If I light a fire, my limbs and other organs shouldn't get burnt.

You are a bad girl, Malu. I'm leaving.

Go if you can. Who wants to travel on a bus with no brakes? It is okay. Even if my grave isn't six feet long, it should be deep, for it must be a place where I can bury all my wayward thoughts.

WARMTH

A seven-year affair, but our families said our gods were different.

I went away with him. We had a place we called our own. Today, he dropped me at my office, planting half a kiss on my lips, and saving the other half for later. Then I got a phone call. I couldn't understand what they were saying. I went to the hospital; they made me sign a lot of forms. They asked me to pay the bills and buy medicines. We returned home together.

The house was filled with uninvited guests. People demanded many things – a white cloth, a towel, a matchbox, myrrh, frankincense. I couldn't pay attention. They held my hand and spoke to me. My legs and back ached from all the running around. I wanted to lie down. It was late evening by the time I dived under my blanket after a bath. The blanket carried the warmth he had left behind. I buried my face into it.

HALF-COOKED

The woman in me hadn't begun to bleed. But I was disturbed. My breasts and lower belly had begun to throb. I wanted to sit in a corner by myself. My body had begun to hate the touch of men. When my body resisted his touch, he grew irritated. The irritation would congeal and refuse to melt. I could understand that. Yet I felt like dumping this body of mine somewhere. Or he could just take my two female parts and leave my smouldering mind behind. I'll use it as a place to stack my wayward thoughts and dreams.

Hearing me mutter, Dr Janaki smiled. Her gentle hands – which had birthed many newborns and were as soft as clouds – touched me, stroked me and pressed my hands. 'There's nothing to worry. It has only been five years. We will do a scan after you get your period.'

I wanted to laugh. I felt a cradle made of red silk swing

inside of me, meant for my butterfly baby. How could she not come? But my cycles had gone awry.

Today is the 31st of December. Another year has passed. I wanted life to move on as swiftly as time. As much as I love life, I grow weary of it at times. I wanted to let off like a pressure cooker whistle, and vomit out everything. Sometimes, I wanted to grow old, grey and wrinkled. I could then walk on the streets as I wanted. No one would stare at my breasts. No one would be curious about the lack of a companion. There would be no interpretations or judgments. I would have freedom from being wanted, freedom to see, hear and do what I desired. I opened the newspaper with such thoughts flooding my mind, only to see news stories about rape and women of all ages being trafficked. I shut down my dreams of expeditions into the unknown.

My next set of wings would sprout while I was on a journey. I would toy with the idea of getting down at a random railway station, without any bags or my phone. I would simply jot down ideas and words that popped up in my mind. I would write them down as poetry:

I should go on a long trip
Without goodbyes,
Without return tickets.

An 'Unidentified Body'
At some remote place!
I wouldn't be I anymore
Without identity cards.

I, who loves to live in my memories,
Can then 'live' in the memories of others.

How would they
Remember me?
Ah! It's interesting.

How would I
Remember me?

I'm ridiculous
I'm far less than I could have been
And I'd like to be otherwise
But I can't seem to help myself.

My English isn't very good. I wasn't a good student. I didn't even know which course I should pick. What did I really know? So my family took an easy decision – to get me married.

I like jotting down sentences I read in books. These last few lines, too, are from a book I had read. As I read them again, the desire to go away grew stronger. I thought about something I had seen a long time ago, when I was travelling on a long-distance train. The train had stopped at a station at night. A heavily pregnant woman sat under the yellow light on the platform. Shabbily dressed, she carried a belly that was the result of someone else's lust. She probably had lice in her hair, I thought, as she incessantly combed it. A man who was watching came up and touched her. She pushed his hand away. He took the comb from her hand and started combing her hair. The woman must have been longing for another human being's touch. She sat as a child would in front of its mother. The comb fell from his hand into her lap. As he picked it up, his hands touched her breasts. She pushed them away. He picked up the comb again. It fell again, and he again picked it up and touched her. This happened many times before he became bold enough to put his hand inside her blouse. He ignored her resistance. Finally, he pulled her into the darkness behind the railway station.

My scream was caught inside my throat. I was the girl with the heavy womb stepping into the wilderness of the night. I wanted to get down and save that woman. I couldn't sleep that night. Even today, I can see her walking into the night. No, I did not want to get off at a strange railway station.

While alone at home, I would think about death (each time, I would be killed by a different disease). The house and I would lie cold till the evening. When the others came home, to the usual routine, to the food, they would be shocked to find me there. They would first grow irritated seeing me lying still, ignoring the work that needed to be done. I would want to tell them: don't bury me! Burn me instead, or I would be as alone under the earth as I am now. What if I were to come alive, if, following the Holy Book, they buried me after wrapping me in a shroud? I would not be able to pick the worms off me. I would suffocate when it rained and the rainwater filled my grave with mud. All my orifices would be stuffed with cotton, and beneath the earth, I would be unable to even cry out if my consciousness were to return. No, no, no, I did not want to be buried! I have to be cremated. Burn me and feed the ashes to the plants in my garden!

Melancholic at the thought of turning into a handful of ash seeping into the roots of my plants, I turned the pages of a weekly. The famous author Sara Joseph had written about this. I didn't even have my own dreams. I made up my mind to not die.

I decided to continue watching the movie I had left halfway the previous day. I could not watch a movie in a single sitting. The wife, daughter and sister in me would get up and block my vision.

Every single moment I spent with you,
Will not be forgotten even on my death bed, O darling!

I don't remember how many times I had already watched this scene from a Tamil movie. I don't think there can be a more romantic scene. They lay together with their heads nestled on each other's shoulders. Beneath her dishevelled clothes, beneath her black sari, was her fair skin, invisible to the eye. Her tresses fell on his bare chest. The scene had everything that love demanded: ecstasy, passion, pain. He rained as poetry from the heights of passion. She was a woman who had left behind her land and her people for his poetry. Even as she stood bathed in his love, his fingers touched a teardrop. I too touched her salty tears with his fingers.

Spoken Tamil has a disarming charm. 'O Dravida, let me put my head on your chest that's been darkened under the yoke of Aryan rule. Could you speak to me in this tongue about your love for me? Will you snub the female sprouts in my womb? Will you end them with rice corns, will you drown them in a bucket of water, or will you put them in wet towels so they grow feverish and perish?'

I couldn't finish watching this movie even today. I turned it off.

The curry was still on the stove while I daydreamed. I wonder how many times the cooker had whistled. If it had whistled thrice, the salt, tomato and the ginger-garlic paste would have blended well with the potatoes and chicken. If it were the fourth whistle, the chicken would be overcooked.

Everything must be cooked well to taste great, or else it would turn out to be like me: half-cooked.

GANDHARVAM: A SECRET MARRIAGE

You won't believe me if I tell you, or you may say I am making it all up. I don't have the skills to describe it. Certain things have to be experienced. They cannot be told. My vocabulary is limited as it is, but I will try nonetheless.

I was in the last year of undergraduation. I remember the dark smell of the chemistry lab. Students were talking about the young unmarried teacher in boring classes. I argued that the dimpled maths teacher was more handsome, with his winning smile. The boys in my class were pathetic and pitiable. The boys studying Commerce were the smart lot. Someone would always be sitting under the shade of the 'Commerce Tree'. Sometimes, it would be the ones I fancied or had a crush on, with his or her newest fancy. It was also a time when my new hairstyle had become a rage (I had tied up my long hair and created a small wave in front, holding it up with a thousand hairpins. It was worth spending all that time in front of the mirror, judging by the attention I got!). I knew they called me a 'Russian beauty'. On the other hand, there were constant reminders for me to stop bunking classes, as it was my final year.

Well, if I go on like this, there will be no order to the story. I wanted to talk about something else.

We were four friends. One of us had a stomach ache (the usual!) and hadn't come to class. Another hadn't returned after going home for the weekend. The third was a dimwit adjusting the calculations in her record book. The last date to submit was today, a Monday, which wasn't a good day.

My gang wasn't here. The boy had gone to play cricket so I lost a golden opportunity to flirt with him. I decided to miss the last hour of classes and go home. There was no one around as I walked to the bus stop. The principal must have finished his rounds. I reached the culvert and saw a young boy, around thirteen or fourteen, near the bamboo hedge. An ink stain had spread over his shirt pocket. A broken button hung from his shirt. A faint shadow of a stubble grew over his lips. His penetrating eyes that sat below thick eyebrows and a broad forehead pierced me. Pointing his tapering fingers at me, he said, 'You are mine! Wait for me.'

I wanted to burst out laughing. I wanted to pinch his ears and tell him we had a boy of his age at home and this is what I did to him when he annoyed me.

But…

Why didn't I say anything? Why did I find his nails perfect? Boys usually didn't have such beautiful nails. Why was I sure colours seeped from his fingers and created art?

He turned to look at me. His gaze! Oof! I didn't know where it pierced me. His hair flopped onto his forehead. One of his teeth was slightly crooked. Mischief danced in a corner of his eye. Was the smile on his lips meant only for me? A song meant for me?

What was I even thinking? Just because a twit of a boy said something? I didn't falter even when seniors teased me. I lived in a world of my own, filled with inferiority complexes and dreams. Don't tell my friends that I lived in solitude. To them, I was quite chatty, and made friends easily. No one had seen the ocean of loneliness within me.

I could have said so many things to him… yet…

I don't remember how long I stood there. I don't remember how I got home that day. Did I walk the 25 kilometres to my home or did I get on a bus?

Amma said I fell on my bed when I got home. She told me the air was hot around me but when she touched me, I was cold. I don't know how many days I spent in bed. I was given medicines at first as they assumed I was ill. When that didn't work, they started conducting pujas. I only have faint memories of those days.

He appeared in my dream and told me, 'I just asked you to wait for me. Why are you cooped up inside your house? Go to college.'

I went to college the next day. I copied down notes. When I drew Benzene and Toluene and their bonds, I wanted to fill them with colour. My fingers had suddenly grown long. I wanted to hum a song.

My friend came back after winning the cricket match. When he started talking to me, I wondered why his eyes looked lifeless. I was irritated his hair did not flop over his forehead. I didn't want to continue talking to him.

My friends started cracking more jokes. My family began to ask me about my day. New clothes filled my cupboard. There were long phone calls from my home to my friends. My aunts and cousins arrived. They gave me company and spoke to me at length. I acted as if they had a problem and listened patiently as I comforted them.

They wondered whether I had been possessed by a demi-god. The local superstition was that young virgin girls were likely to become possessed.

'Did something scare her? Remember Radha's daughter, Shobha?'

'Has someone cast a spell on her? Times are bad.'

'There was nothing wrong with her when she went to college on Monday. Her friends said there were no problems in class either.'

'Then?'

My mother wept when someone suggested a psychiatrist.

'She's an unmarried girl.'

Even as all this was raging around me, I continued to attend class every day, as if I were just a body whose soul had been removed. I conducted titration and salt analyses in the lab. I wrote my exam and got a first class.

Now what?

He appeared in my dream again. He had grown thinner. He told me if one mixed leftover rice from the previous day with chilies and ate it for breakfast and ran to class, one would lose weight. He showed me yellow leaves falling into a cold tomb. We devoured the smell of the earth wet with rain. He ran his fingers through the numerous talismans around my waist that had become wet in the rain. He asked me, 'Why do you need all this? I will buy you a silver chain to hug your hips.' When he went back, he told me, 'You have to learn literature.'

While my friends spent hours in the laboratory, stories and poems kept me company. No one said anything at home. My mother started fasting more. My father's hair and beard turned greyer with each passing day.

You must be imagining that I looked like a wreck with lifeless eyes. But I had a flame that burned bright where my soul should have been. The heat of that flame turned my cheeks red, made my eyes open wider. Young admirers came to me, willing to be moths around that flame. He laughed out loud in my dreams. Oh god! His laughter! I looked at him in open-mouthed wonder. I scribbled in my notebook. My walls were filled with my artwork. I sought new meanings in songs. I travelled from one book to the next.

My uncles, aunts, neighbours and their spouses, and even our maid, Susheela, brought wedding proposals for me as if they feared I would remain a spinster. The grooms were perfect – handsome young men from good families. I served them tea and snacks. They liked the quiet girl – so well-brought up.

But the girl…

'I want to study more.' (Till *he* comes, I meant.)

Nothing happened. The climax was quite expected. There was emotional blackmail. My father had chest pain. My mother was in tears. She aped the weeping mothers in the movies.

The usual maroon sari and ornaments. The jasmine flowers in my hair were pinned down with a thousand pins, as if someone was taking revenge. I felt the wedding pandal was erected right above my head. I left my body to them and stood aside. I couldn't ask him why he hadn't come for my wedding. I couldn't find him.

After the festivities were over, the husband asked me, 'Were you interested in sports?'

'No.'

'Dance, then?'

'No.'

He must have been troubled by a hymen that didn't birth a spot of blood.

Between brushing my teeth twice a day, between opening and closing a door, between breakfast and dinner, my days and nights repeated themselves.

The boy arrived at dawn. He held my hand and took me to the river. His chest smelt of tulsi. My breasts throbbed. The fire on my lips broke into a flame. My body blossomed, and I rained. He was drenched in it. Beneath the river that blanketed us, he entered my soul like a thousand blissful fire-sticks. The sun dawned that day in a river that I had turned vermilion.

'Are you on your period?'

'No.'

'What is this then?'

When I got up, an exquisite pain enveloped my body. There was a spot of blood on my clothes and sheet. My wet hair smelt of tulsi.

PULP ROMANCE AND THE EPILOGUE

I didn't recognize Sandeep when he stood in front of me. I was checking the accounts at the shop and making a list of books we needed to order next month. Sandeep used to come in the evenings after work, and we would talk till it was time to close the shop for the night. A few others would participate in our conversation.

Nowadays, when we were alone, he would only speak about Lekha. After listening to him wax eloquently on this topic, I felt I could write her biography! He described the bus stop where he had first met her as if it were a scene from a movie. 'The very green plants and the very vibrant flowers' was how he described the place. He acted as if he was seeing the ubiquitous Siam weed, which we locally called 'Communist Pacha', for the first time in his life. I saw bits and pieces of Lekha even before meeting her. I saw the crescent mark on her neck, the burn scar on her right wrist (from when she cooked for the first time), her even teeth, the moving ocean in her eyes, and her soft feet. Sandeep had become an ardent fan of Padmarajan movies and stories by then. When he spoke, he invariably began with, 'Lekha says' or 'Lekha thinks.'

Sandeep looked as if he had been struck by a tsunami. He looked dishevelled. I knew whatever he wanted to tell me was something tragic. I thought I should take him aside, hold his hand, and ask him what the matter was. But I started thinking about his past as if it were a joke. It seemed to be the 'comic relief' I had learnt about in literature classes. Though I had sat in class only to see the way the teacher Shashikala draped her sari, I remembered such things. Was there any other reason why I still remembered the guard from the hell scene in *Macbeth*? The day when she had explained this scene, she had worn a blue sari that was more transparent than her other saris. I remember the breeze that crossed the veranda, and Gopi who pinched me saying he would have to put a heavy dictionary on his lap. Laughter gurgled in my throat, but I stopped it seeing Sandeep's face. I got up and led him to the bookshelves. He pressed my hand in silence. I felt his pain and grew anxious. 'What's wrong? Tell me.'

Sandeep said, 'When I met Lekha, I realized that a man became complete only when a woman came into his life. Not that my life was boring before I met her. I had my bit of fun – evenings spent with friends, watching movies, etc. But when a woman enters your life, you experience the happiness of living for someone else. I have already told you I saw Lekha for the first time on a rainy evening. A girl walked ahead of me as I walked to the bus stop from work. Curious as any man would be, I looked at her. Her beautiful feet, with anklets around them, were getting wet in the rain. Raindrops caught in her hair glistened. It was a usual romantic scene. When I got closer, I thought I heard someone humming a song. I wondered if background music was playing like in the movies. Just as I thought I was imagining things, I realized the girl was singing. She looked as happy as a frog seeing the rain after a long time. "Even silence is sweet, in this moonlit rain..." she hummed.

'I was impressed by her boldness, the way she claimed the world as hers. We met a couple of times after that. We fell in love. She was a good student. She came from a poor family so she did part-time jobs, including taking tuitions, to pay for her studies. Her family's circumstances were dire, so I decided to sponsor her teacher-training course because she wanted to be independent. Even though I had my responsibilities – a sister who was of marriageable age – and other demands on my purse, I decided to do it for her. My mother asked me to stop romancing her and instead get married. But I wanted her life to be free of worries while she studied. That was the best part of my life, until the day Lekha called me home. "Sandeep, come home. My parents have gone to Guruvayoor for a wedding. Megha and Nandu are in school. Come over for lunch."

'To be honest, my male thoughts turned spicy. She was mine, so it didn't feel wrong. I felt weak as I sat in office. Time seemed to move slowly. I thought about her boldness in inviting me home. When I reached her house, I noticed she too was nervous. I was ecstatic as she served me food that she had cooked. I relished every morsel. She took me to her room after lunch. I felt a slight tremor in my legs. I grew worried if she could hear my heart thud noisily. I barely noticed her neatly arranged room. Suddenly, she held my face in her hands and said, "Do whatever you want to do. I am in love with someone else but that doesn't mean I love you any less."

'I didn't hear anything else. My mind was empty when I walked out. I wandered aimlessly. I am not myself anymore. You tell me, what should I do now?'

My eyes began to flood when Sandeep asked me this question, utterly helpless, and holding my hand tightly. It was as if someone had emptied the vessel in which I had stored all the words I knew. I didn't know what to tell him. Lekha must have been joking, or they may have had a fight. But before I could ask him anything, the managing director walked in to discuss the book fair that was scheduled for next week.

I got caught up in work and didn't see Sandeep leave. When I tried to call him, his phone was switched off. We looked for him everywhere. We couldn't bear to visit his house when his mother asked us with tear-filled eyes whether we knew where he was. Fearing the black-and-white obituary pages, my fingers didn't touch the newspaper. Every ring of the phone filled me with both hope and anxiety. There were days when my left eye and my right eye twitched alternately: a bad omen!

The third day after Sandeep disappeared, I found his mobile phone among the books at work. Some of our friends muttered it was another bad omen. When I saw the phone, I was convinced he had left out of his own volition. Every time we met, our friends cursed Lekha in turn.

'Everyone talks about women being exploited, but what about the men destroyed by women?' We could hear Louis grinding his teeth as he thought about his wife.

'Women can never be trusted.' Ashokan unleashed his anger on Lekha thinking about his mother who had remarried after his father's death.

'You shouldn't pursue women. They will never give us any importance. You should demand a huge dowry and get married. Even if she isn't pretty, it doesn't matter. And if you are in love, get married quickly instead of paying her college fees.' Divakaran spat out into the compound as if he were spitting on women.

'He was a fool. Not just because he paid her fees, but because he walked out silently when she told him everything. If it had been me, I would have fucked not just her but her mother as well.' Words turned sour and stank in this all-male conclave.

I suddenly thought of a joke I had received on WhatsApp: On her wedding night, a bride confessed that she was in love with someone else. The groom said, 'At least let me make some use of the money I have spent on the *pandal*. You can leave tomorrow.'

Koya, who had been silent till then, said, 'Humans are unpredictable. You can never know what they will desire or when. So every day, before I reach home, I call her to say I'm on my way home and that she should have my tea and snacks ready, or I ask her if she needs anything from the store. If she has invited anyone home, this will give him enough time to leave. Or at least she will be happy that I called to enquire. Why should one live in pain, witnessing unsavoury sights? We have such short lives, so why not be happy?'

Everyone fell silent, realizing the deep philosophy in Koya's words. The friends applied a sudden brake to their thoughts about one's own philandering and then realizing the person at home too would have similar desires.

What Lekha had to say:

Days after Sandeep left, Lekha came to meet me. I was furious when I saw her. Wicked wretch! Wondering why she had come to see me, I pretended to be busy. She patiently waited for me. I finally yielded. We sat across each other with cups of coffee. Without beating about the bush, she began, 'I have come to you because you are Sandeep's closest friend. I know all of you blame me. Even my mother refuses to speak to me now. No one understood me as Sandeep did. I had the freedom to speak my mind when we were together. And even though he can be quite possessive, I never hid anything from him. I liked a classmate. You can't decide whom you fall in love with. When I got to know him, I realized I couldn't forget him. I could walk away from that relationship out of gratitude to Sandeep. But that resentment would surface after we married. What if I started to feel it was simply gratitude that made me marry Sandeep? I didn't want to lie in my husband's arms thinking about another man. I couldn't live sheltering a lie. I couldn't do that to Sandeep.'

I sat for a long time after Lekha left. I felt she was right, but I also wished she wasn't so honest.

Slowly everyone went back to their own lives. Then one day, I received a phone call from an unfamiliar number. It was Sandeep. I felt that I was listening to the story of a B-grade movie. He had decided to commit suicide, then he wanted to sell his kidney to give money to his girlfriend and his family, and finally he had begun to wander around hungry and desolate. He had returned and had shut himself up inside his room. He grew his beard long and behaved like Devdas. He kept playing the same sad songs over and over till his father reached the end of this tether and bought him a new collection of sad songs.

I had just picked up a weekly to read on a quiet, rainy afternoon at the shop. The cover story was on the relevance of Marxism. As I glanced through its pages, I thought of Sandeep and Lekha. Like a few new-generation journalists who realized Marxism was irrelevant, Lekha too knew that love was short-lived and had left behind her romance to die. On the other hand, Sandeep was like a stubborn unrealistic communist who had decided to embrace the ideology. As I was thinking of this comparison, a girl walked in, drenched in rain.

'Bro, a sexy gal, dripping wet, just came in and is asking me for *The Arabian Nights*. Shall I give it to her? (It's just me and her in the shop right now.)'

I picked up my phone to send this message to my boys' gang with a winking emoticon at the end.

BUTTERFLIES BECOME CATERPILLARS

This is Madhusoodanan Nair. And his name is the only thing he shares with the famous poet. This man can't even appreciate a movie song. Money is his God. For him, his job, his position, the earth, sand and water are all ways to earn money. He is fifty-three, and both his children are abroad. They are paying back, in instalments, the money he has spent to educate them.

It was a day like any other. He was reading the newspaper. Rukmini was busy making breakfast. Casting his eyes over the list of rapes and the episodes of pimping, he sighed. A son pimping his mother; a father selling his daughter; a teacher hawking his student; and a boyfriend fixing a price for his girlfriend!

Rukmini saw Madhu staring at her while she brought the chapati and kurma from the kitchen. She was taken aback. Not even during his youth had he looked at her in such a manner. These days, when he felt like it, he would indulge in sex in a lackadaisical way.

Butterflies fluttered within her. A smile twinkled on the dimple in her cheek. She took a long bath. Looking at her grey hair peeping from within the tattered curtain of henna, she decided to go to the beauty parlour the very next day. She decided to use the money her husband had given her to buy fish to dye her hair. She discarded her stained nightie for a sari.

Chewing on his chapati, Madhusoodanan thought, 'The bitch eats too much and her belly hangs out. If she had been in better shape, I could have made some money!'

RIGOR MORTIS

I wanted to laugh when I saw Ramachandran. One leg was almost touching the ground, and his right hand was raised as if he was about to get up. I thought of a game children played: if someone called out 'Statue', you had to freeze in whatever position you were. If you moved, you lost the game and got punished. Raman looked as if someone had called out 'Statue' as he was about to stand up. It was indeed a suitable game for a sixty-three-year-old!

Dawn was nearly here. I had been sitting in the same place for more than three hours. Raman didn't show any signs of waking up. The sweat on his brow had dried. His body had turned slightly cold now. Long ago, he had once gone cold like this in school, when he had inadvertently brushed against Remani from 10B. At that time, blood rushed to both his toes and his head, as if a valve had been opened. That day, he wrote in his diary, 'It felt as if there was burning coal on the palm of my hand.'

He had come a long way from the time his moustache first made an appearance and Remani's breasts bloomed; he did not wake up even when Remani's name was mentioned.

The newspaper boy rang the bell on his bicycle. Families began to wake up. A rusty gate creaked somewhere, a pressure cooker whistled, a child was being woken up and scolded. I heard the honking of a school bus, the strain of a song from a radio, and someone trying to start a scooter. The smell of sambhar wafted in. But the man who would shout at Vanaja if breakfast wasn't ready by 8.30 a.m. was lying still.

The sounds of the morning began to fade. I could now hear a woman washing clothes. I went out of the room. Vanaja's absence was evident. Dirty clothes and dirty plates were scattered around. There was food in the kitchen that had been bought from a restaurant. I realized Raman was a stickler for cleanliness only when his mother or wife was around.

Vanaja should not have walked out. After all, she had known him for so long. He must have shouted at her thinking she was used to it and would never leave. A quarrel may have begun from a silly reason. Both of them may have even forgotten the cause of the quarrel by now. It would have become something different by then: something sewn up by bitter egos, something complicated and unnecessarily blown up.

It had been two weeks since Vanaja left. She hadn't called, and Raman's male ego had prevented him from calling her.

The smell of mustard seeds, curry leaves and shallots being sautéed in coconut oil told me it was afternoon. Whom could I call? I wished someone would ring the bell. I walked around the house in despair. I don't know how much time I spent thinking.

Suddenly, I heard the sound of children returning from school. A while later, I heard them play cricket – hitting a six, getting run out. This was followed by advertisements and soaps on TV. Then the shouts and screams from political pundits on news channels. It must be past 10. Homes were sliding back into sleep. But no one was curious enough to ask why the lights hadn't come on in this house.

In the darkness, the light from the torch near Raman's bed seemed like a reptile. There are times when man, who prides himself on conquering the mountains and the moon, becomes completely helpless. Look at Raman now. He can't even call for help. Just as you need help to be born, you need help to leave this earth decently too. It has been twenty-four hours that I have been watching over him. Unless someone comes, I can't do anything. I expected a phone call, but even that hope turned futile. She wouldn't call in all likelihood.

I sat on the sofa and picked up the TV remote. Though

quite innocuous, this thing was enough to set off a squabble, like on the night it happened.

After finishing all her chores at night, Vanaja cleaned the kitchen and sat on the sofa to watch the movie *Manichitrathazhu*. Raman walked in and snatched the remote from her. 'You women are all the same. You watch the same movies and TV serials over and over. You watch the advertisements in between and start whining for a new induction cooker, or you demand gold jewellery like the kind Kareena Kapoor wears for Akshaya Tritiya.' He then switched the channel and started watching the news.

'There is a mad, fiery woman within me at all times, one who seeks vengeance, who wants to roam free, and yet here I am, confined to daily chores of cooking and cleaning!' Vanaja's soliloquy was astounding. She stared at him so fiercely that her eyes almost blazed fire. The very next day, she left the house when Raman shouted at her for not having washed the underwear he wanted to wear. Well, you couldn't really blame Raman. He had grown up watching his mother do this for his father, so naturally he expected his wife to do the same.

When Raman was a boy, his mother would rub coconut oil mixed with turmeric on him before bathing him so that he would become fairer. But now, his skin had turned dark. How much time did it take for worms to eat our bodies, bodies that we nurture with fragrant soaps and perfumes?

This fly is buzzing around and irritating me.

I heard the thud of the newspaper. The boy must have seen yesterday's newspaper is still lying on the veranda. Why doesn't he ring the bell and find out why? Why don't the men who join Raman on his morning walk come looking for him? Why can't they call at least? Why can't his daughter be bothered to enquire?

The radio next door blasted a sad song from a movie. It's been two days since I entered Raman's room. It is stinking now. The room is filled with flies. The blood that had oozed from his nose and mouth has congealed.

Raman was twelve when his father died. When he saw the cotton balls stuffed in his father's nostrils, he grew worried. What would his father do if he had the urge to sneeze? He suspected they had stuffed cotton into his father's nose to prevent him from breathing and coming back to life... He must have understood now that the cotton was used to stop the bleeding.

Did I hear a footfall outside? No. I must have imagined it. I have been longing for someone to come in. I am even getting used to the smell of putrefying flesh. But no, there were indeed people outside, quite a few of them in fact. They were walking around the house, talking in whispers.

A police jeep arrived after a while. Oh Raman, you are lucky! Or are you? No one has seen you so dishevelled. You always took care to wear sparkling clean clothes. I heard them debating whether to kick the door open. Someone said that the house owner must be informed.

They smashed open the window and entered the house. The police arrived first, then the neighbours. They had deferred their daily bustle.

As the number of people increased, so did the number of stories: murder, suicide, his wife leaving him. The ones who had arrived first authoritatively narrated the stories to the latecomers. Someone brought one of Raman's relatives who lived in the vicinity. That man did not even know Raman's daughter's name. Once again, with their fingers on their respective noses, they lamented over times such as the present, when people lived such isolated lives. A girl from a TV channel came by. Baby, an auto driver, exclaimed at the plight of old people left alone at home. Ganesh and his friend demanded ₹500 for alcohol and ₹5,000 to move the body before cleaning the room. The police officers asked the house owner to pay them and started to prepare the report. As they looked around for the person who had first seen the body and the one who had called the station, the crowd slowly melted away.

Pouring liquor down their throats, Ganesh and his gang moved in. Even Raman's mother, who had carried him on her hip while feeding him rice and ghee so that he would put on some weight, wouldn't recognize him now.

The house owner anxiously asked someone over the phone whether he should deduct the ₹5,000 from the advance or whether he should take more money and get the room painted over. His anxiety increased when he remembered the constable telling him that he wouldn't get a new tenant as the vaastu of the house spelt death for the owner. He was surprised when the same policeman told him the location of the house was excellent and asked whether he was thinking of letting it out.

A car came by and stopped in the portico. You could hear the beginnings of a wail. Raman and I were a single body, but I can't be here any longer. I am not a soul that can bear tears and wails, especially as I had watched Raman rotting away for these past two days.

What would Vanaja be thinking of now? That you won't give me peace even in death? That you have humiliated me by dying and rotting in this way? For the first time, she wouldn't complain about not having a house of their own. She would want to leave behind these memories as quickly as possible. The nervous young girl whom I had married, the one who didn't know what to call me, who had shyly asked me to buy her a yellow-and-blue sari to wear on her friend's wedding, whose heart beat against mine when I held her close – would she have a grain of love left for me now?

I would like to know.

MADNESS

When madness wound itself around her legs, Rajmohana would start living many lives. She would forget Paloma, her father and the life they had together.

Today, she was Chiminy, who was just eight years old. She would start blinking when she clutched the lollipop her uncle gave her. This earned her the name 'Chiminy', meaning 'the girl who blinked'. As she was burdened with chores in her old ancestral house, her mother didn't notice Chiminy walking with her legs apart. Nor did she notice her daughter's blooming breasts. No one noticed when she went missing for hours, nor did they see her sitting in a corner with the lollipop still in its wrapper, her eyes blinking. They didn't see the strands of coconut fibre or the bits of hay that got caught in her hair at times; they didn't notice the smell of milk had left her and that she had started smelling of the dust in the attic.

Rajmohana felt suffocated. She got up coughing. She was sweating. She started blinking. When she got her breath back, she drank some water and walked to Devamma's room with her legs wide apart. She opened the old trunk and started searching for something.

'What are you looking for? What do you want now?'

Rajmohana picked up an old album and pointed to a black-and-white photograph. 'Who is this?' she asked in Hindi. She forgot the Malayalam her mother had insisted on teaching her, as well as the painful pinches she had received on her thighs.

Devamma adjusted her glasses and held up the photo to light. Then she sighed.

'This is Chiminy, isn't it? Padmini Aunty's daughter. We were around the same age. She may have been a bit younger. She was ill. She would always sit in a corner and blink her eyes. She wouldn't join us in our games. Then she died suddenly. No one knew what was wrong with her…'

Rajmohana wanted to point out that Chiminy's death wasn't sudden. It had taken some time to come – her mouth and nose had been held closed till she gasped for air, and the weight on her had become limp and unbearable. Death was slimy, she thought.

She drew water from the well and bathed. But the cool well water couldn't quench the fire that burnt within her. She discarded the towel as she remembered her aunt's husband's smug face when he said the towel smelt of her. She didn't use the towel to dry her body. It dried by itself.

'Amma, let us return to Delhi. I don't like it here.'

'Who is there in Delhi? Your course is over too. You can look for a job here.'

'I want to go to my father. You know where he is. Tell me!'

'He must be with that Tamil woman. Go and ask her. Great intellectuals.' She spat out her ire.

As her mother walked away, she wanted to call out, 'If you could go to a strange city 24 years ago, it is far easier for me now.'

But she didn't say it. Instead, she thought of Rihan. She saw in his restless eyes love pouring down like falling Chinar leaves.

When she felt like crying, she went to the steps near the pond. She couldn't cry inside the house. She thought of her dad's beard brushing against her forehead. A hug from him could melt all her sorrows away. She wished her mother hadn't boarded that train. She only knew the stories her father had told her. Her mother had never told her stories about their romance. Nor did the daughter tell her mother about the man she loved.

Nirmala met Pranoy Banerjee on a train. She had moved from children's literature to philosophy and from religion to the fiery speeches of Communists. She had attained the strength to resist all kinds of reactionary ideologies. She was returning from Hyderabad, where she had gone for a study tour, when she met Pranoy on the train. Pranoy was on his way to Kerala as an invited speaker at the Communist party conclave after a camp in Hyderabad.

Can you fall in love with someone you meet on a train? Would she elope with him? When Rajmohana expressed her surprise, Pranoy laughed. 'She must have mistaken me for Pranoy Roy upon seeing my beard.'

'Tell me, Dada, tell me about your romance.'

Pranoy would then turn into Rumi:

The minute I heard my first love story
I started looking for you, not knowing
How blind that was
Lovers don't finally meet somewhere
They're in each other all along.

Rajmohana imagined they must have eloped like lovers in Bollywood movies. He must have sent her a train ticket, and she must have left her house. By the time the background song ended, she, that is Rajmohana alias Paloma, would be in the cradle. She remembered that her mother never really liked the Mani Ratnam movie

Bombay, which had a similar scene. The moment she saw that movie on TV, she would turn off the set or change the channel.

'Why are you sitting here at twilight when it is time to light the lamp? Is this what you do back home?'

It was the maid Kalyani amma, with feudal servility coursing through her veins.

'I'm waiting to see your gandharva, your divine lover. You bathe in the evenings to meet him, right?'

'My gandharva would have reached home by now, dead drunk, and on all fours. Go inside.'

Rajmohana thought it was better to have a phantom lover who blossomed at night and left in the morning. Marriage would tire out even demi-gods.

Dada had once told her, 'In her mind, your mother is still going around the Tulsi plant at her house.'

Dada always had people around him: students, activists, Natyamanch members. Dada had strong convictions. He was convinced one should never stop resisting fascism no matter how weak one's voice may be. He ignored the threats. When Nirmala became pregnant, she gravitated towards her family. Pranoy had nurtured the name 'Paloma', but when Nirmala returned from Kerala with the baby, she had a birth certificate for 'Rajmohana'.

Nirmala had wanted to name her daughter 'Devayani', after her grandmother, but the great writer VKN's stories made her choose 'Rajmohana'. Nirmala didn't know then that her daughter would publish her works under the name 'Paloma'.

The baby took her first faltering steps right in the middle of Dada's circle of friends. Hearing them call him Pranoda, Pranoyda and Dada, she too started to call him Dada. Her mother's scolding couldn't change Dada to Acha. The gods that Nirmala had stubbornly arranged on her shelves didn't seem to help her.

'Mohana, please give this *kanji* to your great-grandmother,' her aunt, who didn't want to take a break from her TV serial, told her. Her great-grandmother sat up with outstretched legs on her bed when Rajmohana's walked in. She didn't seem to sense Rajmohana presence.

'Hi, young girl, come on, get up. Don't you want to hit a century?' Even at 98, her great-grandmother looked glamorous, Rajmohana thought. If her wrinkles could be ironed out, she would look divine.

'Seetha Lakshmi, you must be careful.'

'Ammamma, I am Mohana.'

'Seetha, you are at a dangerous age. Don't ever go out alone. Everyone goes to sleep after lunch here. This house sleeps as well. You must come and lie down next to me then.'

'Ammamma, should I call Devamma?'

'Who is Devamma?'

'Don't you remember? Devamma is your daughter, Seetha Lakshmi.'

'Who changed her name?'

'I don't know. Everyone calls her Devamma – Dev mama's amma.'

'Seetha must have died. I know. I didn't breastfeed her. I didn't hold her close. How could I? I was mad then.'

'Oh! Seetha married and had four children. I am her second daughter Nirmala's daughter.'

'But you don't look like you are one of us. What is your name?'

'Paloma.'

'Isn't that what that foul-smelling oil is called?' She sat up and stirred the gruel, but did not take in a single mouthful.

'Seetha, you must be so angry with me?' Devayani asked, looking Rajamohana straight in the eye. Her eyes filled with tears to compensate for the milk she had denied her daughter.

'I was my mother's fourteenth child. She lost two children after me. Amma wouldn't have had a moment to close her legs.' She burst out laughing, but her eyes wept. 'My oldest sister's son was two years older than me. Do you see this scar on my forehead? I fell in the bathroom when he tried to grab me. Look, blood is dripping into the gruel!'

She pushed away the plate. Rajmohana was scared. She couldn't bring herself to move.

'Do you know, only lifeless objects have honour and dignity? This house, this family – I don't have it, I shouldn't. The midwife plucked it out as easily as we knock a papaya off the tree. When that Brahmin came to marry me, he saw my scared, trembling body, and left. The next to arrive was the Kshatriya, a Nair. He fought a battle before he left. He broke into my narrow and tight body and gifted you to me, though I tore his back with my nails. One day, I left his mattress outside.* You can't be at war forever. I was worried whether they would pluck you out as well. So I didn't tell anyone about you. As I was giving birth to you, those who had gone before you stood around me. They were neither male nor female, but bathed in blood, they screamed, "Mother!"

'Shutting my eyes, I crawled through the door of madness. That is why I didn't hold you close, my child. Did you ever love me?'

She shook Rajmohana in her madness. As Rajmohana peeled her fingers away and rushed out, she heard her great-grandmother say, 'Do you want to live my life? The

---

* This was a custom to indicate divorce. The man will no longer be allowed to visit her.

life of Devayani, who had hair that touched her knees and full bloomed breasts?'

Rajmohana ran to her room, pulled the pillow over her head, and lay quietly, shutting her ears. She feared that her great-grandmother hadn't closed her door of madness.

The bathroom near the well had a floor made of dark stone and carried the smell of a variety of sweat and urine. A young girl stood inside, wondering where she had hurt herself when she saw the blood on her petticoat. The child, who had been hurt without any pain, who had bled without a wound, cried that she didn't want to grow up.

When Rajmohana ran out, a few people had already gathered in the front yard, their eyes fixed on a screen erected between the areca nut trees. When she went closer, she saw a row of dead bodies laid out. The newsreader had been talking about encounter killings and Maoists. Pranoda's chest, where she once rested her head, was smeared with blood. Beyond that were Rihan's eyes, as still as the Dal Lake.

When Rajmohana opened her eyes to the darkness, she smelt blood. She thought she was lying down with the dead bodies. When she realized it was a dream, she sat up and laughed till she cried. Then she rang Sarayu. Sarayu, who smelled of marigolds, who would come home wearing a cotton sari, a bag flung over her shoulder. She gifted books and thoughts to Rajmohana. She would recite her Tamil poems. But she stopped coming home when she realized there were volcanic eruptions at home after she left.

Rihan, too, was the same. He was Dada's student. Nirmala used to like him, too. She would make jasmine-white pancakes for him. Rihan found them fascinating and loved to eat them. But when Nirmala learnt of her daughter's growing affection for him and learnt his surname, her face darkened. Rihan, too, stopped visiting.

Rajmohana first met Rihan at Dada's theatre camp. Dada was remaking *Romeo and Juliet,* adapting it to contemporary reality, when love was translated as Jihad and lovers were hunted down. When the boy selected to play Romeo backed out due to parental pressure, Rihan stepped in. As the day of the performance got closer, Rajmohana stepped in to teach Rihan the dialogues. They spent many days together. Rihan was a man of few words. He would look into her eyes when she spoke. When Rajmohana started listing out the faults of the girl who played Juliet, Dada sang a ghazal:

Isn't it my love for him,
that throbs in my half-shut eyes?
Though it's muffled,
So beats my heart.

When Nirmala walked in, he stopped singing. Rajmohana pretended to answer a call and walked to the veranda, then to the garden. The flowers turned red when they touched her cheeks.

Despite the threats, the play was a success. When it was time to say goodbye, Rihan was silent as usual. Rajmohana stood quietly, playing with her dupatta. He held her face and kissed her on the lips. His kiss told her everything he wanted to say. Mohana was rooted to the spot when Dada walked in. When Dada touched her, she hugged him and said Rihan's lips were as red as Kashmiri chillies, and faintly spicy. Dada kissed her on the forehead. If it had been her mother, she knew she would have felt the heat of tabasco peppers.

The voice on the phone told her Sarayu's number did not exist. Rajmohana felt anger rise inside her. Why had they come away without looking for Dada?

In his columns, Pranoy railed against things he did not approve of. There were rumours that the university would take action against him on account of some of his columns. He didn't pay any heed when his friends warned him the government had changed and there were people who were more loyal to the ruler than the ruler himself.

They told him about hushed-up murders and cooked-up cases, but Dada stood strong and upright.

One December evening, when Dada didn't get home at his usual time, Rajmohana called him. But she kept hearing that his phone was switched off or out of coverage area. Nirmala sneered at her, saying he may be having 'intellectual discussions' with the Tamil woman. Her regret at having to discard her studies for a lover came out in the form of bitter words.

By that night, the voice over the phone said Dada's number did not exist. Rajmohana rang up many people, but no one had a clear answer. Some of them didn't even answer her calls. Sarayu had been in Chennai for a week as her mother was ill. Rajmohana didn't even care if Dada was with her; she just hoped that he was safe.

Then the police came. They ransacked the house, looking for something. They took away Pranoy Da's files and notes. The officials returned the next day, and the day after. Friends told them it wasn't safe for two women to stay alone. Rajmohana couldn't digest the way some of the policemen looked at her and laughed, saying dirty words about her body.

Dev uncle came that week to take them home. Rajmohana felt suffocated. She continued to call people to enquire about Dada. His friends from the media, who had spoken with great enthusiasm once, stopped answering her calls. They slowly migrated to the safety of silence. They had the freedom to eat, drink, dress up and have sex, so why should they get involved and expose themselves to danger? They wrote columns on newly released blockbusters.

Rajmohana had felt safe when she first arrived in her mother's house. The proximity of people all around offered safety. She kept looking at her phone, expecting Dada to call. As days slipped into months, she saw the door of madness opening and felt afraid to sleep.

The route was unfamiliar. I had said it was getting late and that I wanted to return. There were pigeons on the road. You asked me whether I wanted you to stop the car. As the car slowed down, there was a cloud of pigeons over our heads. As we moved ahead laughing, I could smell you.

Rajmohana woke up from a fragrant dream. She had been able to sleep after many days. She had had a pleasant dream. She felt someone dear to her would arrive that day. She waited for her phone to ring. She kept checking the call log in case she missed a call. By evening, her eyes and mind began to ache. The words from the pages of the book she was reading seemed meaningless. Narcissism on Facebook made her nauseous. Filled with hope, she checked her mail as usual, but it yielded the usual disappointment. There was no mail from Dada. She was surprised to find an invitation to attend a seminar being conducted in a university here. She read through the invitation and the topic of the seminar. As she was about to close the mail, she caught a sentence that said, '*Milna hai*.' We have to meet.

Was it Dada? Rihan?

The seminar was scheduled for next week. She felt the wait would kill her. Those were the longest seven days of her life. She checked her mail three to four times every day. She went for the seminar even though Nirmala didn't want her to. She decided she wouldn't speak to Dada if she met him. He had disappeared without a word and left her in the throes of anxiety. Then she thought she would go away with Dada; she wouldn't come back to Nirmala.

Rihan was waiting at the gate. He had lost weight and had grown a beard. He spotted Rajmohana the moment she entered. Taking her hand in his, Rihan stood without speaking. He didn't have any information about Dada either. Rihan told her Dada had been disturbed by the reactions towards his article on the distortion of history in textbooks. He had told Rihan he was worried about Nirmala and his daughter, but not about himself. Dada had a wide circle of friends, some of whom were abroad too. 'He must be safe, and he will return. He can't stay away from you for too long, Paloma.' Rihan told her he no longer used a phone as everyone was being watched. He felt his name and the place he came from would cause trouble for Paloma.

When she lay in his arms in his room in the guesthouse,

she saw the eight-year-old Chiminy running around. She played hide-and-seek wearing her tiny frock, climbed trees, then matured and got an education with her head held high. She daydreamed with her eyes wide open and lay in her lover's arms without blinking. She was ecstatic that the first time she made love, she smelled of sandalwood. Champak flowers bloomed in her hair, leaving no space for hay or coconut fibres.

Then Devayani arrived. The Brahmin and the Nair massaged fragrant oil into her long tresses. They kissed her feet. They stepped into her depths and rose up. They lovingly stroked her swollen belly.

Rihan raised his head and gasped for air.

O, what madness possessed you!

Rajmohana buried her face in his heart, mumbling that she couldn't live without him, that she would go with him. His stubble grazed her forehead. His arms held her in a warm hug. It reminded her of Dada.

THE RECIPE

At night, we sat on top of the tallest building in our college campus. Vibha used her long skirt as a blanket when we shivered from the cool breeze. I would go there alone when my heart was heavy, when I felt lonely. Late one moonlit night, he started speaking about himself on the terrace. When the memory of the cold body of his grandmother, who had drowned in the well, scorched him, I put my hand over his.

When you are alone, the breeze is your only companion. Below you is the city – a blend of darkness and light. A train filled with light moved through the city.

I liked his untimely journeys. I too wanted to get on that island of light and travel.

I still carry the memory of the light-filled train. I mix that in the batter when I make idlis as soft as petals.

KAGAZ KI KASHTI

It was our final year of the undergraduate programme. The beautiful practice of study holidays had begun. My friends would be there when I reached town. We would roam around and go for movies at times before getting back home. My mother would begin, 'You have exams, yet you don't touch your books.' This was her constant refrain.

I decided: No outings this week.

Those were the days I had befriended Jagjit Singh's ghazals.

It had begun raining in the morning. Amma left for school.

Ye kagaz ki kashti
Ye barish ka paani.

Jagjit Singh's soulful voice continued to sing. I wanted to float paper boats in the rain water.

When my mother returned, eighty paper boats and

Jagjit Singh's voice welcomed her. Amma went inside and took out two hundred-rupee notes and said, 'Go out and meet your friends.'

FEELING SAD

'He's gone!'

'What?'

'Should we not go there?'

As he wrote his leave application, Renjith felt doubtful. Had he imagined the conversation?

He looked at his phone. No, Mathan had indeed called him. Just as he got angry that the bugger hadn't told him anything, Mathan arrived. Toby and Biju were with him. They would pick up Vijay on the way.

He felt the heat in his chest while the body burnt some distance away. Someone said, 'He was asleep when he died. He was lucky. He never troubled anyone.' At that point, Mathan began to weep uncontrollably. They somehow pushed him into the car.

By the time he had downed his third peg, Mathan had started to curse. 'Is dying at 46 lucky?' He was trying to drown the helplessness and insecurity all of them collectively felt.

Geetha and the children were sleeping when Renjith got home. But he couldn't sleep. He felt his frequent headaches, the numbness in his left hand, and the various nameless aches and pains he suffered from stand behind him in the form of Yama's buffalo. Without bathing, he started eating the cold rice and fish curry that had been left in the fridge. He wept as though he wouldn't be around to eat it the next day. The coconut had not been ground properly. His mother did a much better job when she used the grinding stone. As he picked his teeth with a toothpick, he thought he must talk to Geetha about it in the morning. He changed into a lungi and sat down to write a post on Facebook:

Do you remember? How can you remember? You were always like this. You pretend not to know something even when you do. It's okay. Let her be happy in the US. Your sister is like a sister to me.

Molamma, our 'well-endowed' Molamma teacher! I know you will not forget her. Don't you remember how we sat with Mathan when he broke his leg in a bike accident, eating the beef fry with coconut bits his mother had cooked? We wished he would break his other leg as well! We were together when we bunked college, drank liquor and watched X-rated movies in the afternoon. We wrote our exams together, failed together, and then appeared for the supplementary exams together. And now, what have you done?

Renjith wrote without a break, listing out life from his exuberant teens to the gasping forties. He felt the Amarula, which Biju's friend had brought from Africa, turn bitter in his mouth.

'It is past 8. Don't you have work today?'

Geetha shook him awake roughly. He couldn't remember when he had slid into sleep. Though he had a headache, he went to office as he did not want to waste a leave. He called up his friends and said the same things over and over again. Vijay had started drinking from the morning itself. His tongue kept slipping as if it was training in French pronunciation.

When he logged on to Facebook that night, Renjith was shocked. He had received a greater number of likes, comments and shares than ever before. Someone had shared his post on WhatsApp groups as well. It was as if his status had changed within the space of a night. He received a dozen friend requests. He couldn't sleep that night.

The next day, his colleague Rajan collapsed and died. He had two more years before retirement. When they returned from the funeral, his beautiful colleague Menaka, who had accepted his friend request after keeping him waiting for three months, came up to him and asked him to post something about Rajan.

Renjith wrote enthusiastically that night. The first like and comment came from Menaka. He felt thrilled. This post garnered even more likes than the first one. The next day, Menaka told him she had never imagined he could write so well. He wanted to ask her to not address him as 'Sir'. He thought about her till Geetha entered the bedroom reeking of fish and wearing a nightie that was torn near the armpits. He turned over in bed.

He would now rush to Facebook to check whether Menaka's green light was on. To get her to like his posts, he began sharing stuff about HCU and JNU protests. He even wrote at length about a minister's corruption. But that post merely got three likes! Menaka ignored it. *A photograph of a girl brushing her teeth would get 300 likes. My foot!* He thought.

He lost sleep wondering who would die next so that he could write about them. He checked the Contacts list on his phone. When Geetha's name popped up, he had already thought of a couple of paragraphs. Two weeks passed without any deaths. He grew terribly bored. His neighbour Kurian's son, Joby, was admitted to the hospital. The boy often played with his children. The doctors suspected dengue.

That night, imagining Joby's death, he wrote a magnificent obituary. He felt tears welling up when he read it himself. He imagined the impact it would have on Menaka. That same night, Geetha said they ought to visit Joby at the hospital.

When he saw Joby lying in the hospital bed, he once again thought about his obituary and its impact on Menaka. He felt disappointed when Molly said that though Joby had high fever, the doctors had confirmed it wasn't dengue. He wondered whether he should send the post to Menaka's inbox instead of letting it go waste.

Kurian had gone to the bank. Molly said that although the hospital was expensive, the treatment had been excellent. She told them how she had been taunted by her in-laws when she had failed to conceive and how her prayers had been answered after seven years. She continued to stroke her son's hand as she spoke. He remembered his two children, followed by a miscarriage, and how his friends had taunted him saying even his underwear could impregnate Geetha. This went on till Geetha's mother took her to the hospital and got her tubes tied.

Geetha told him, 'Please wait here. We are going to the canteen. Molly hasn't eaten anything.'

Hearing the funeral songs from Kurian's house, he sat down in front of his computer, ready to post the obituary, and prayed that the first comment would come from Menaka.

MENSTRUAL COUPÉ

A panting and sweating Subaida reached the station just as the announcement rang out that the train was expected to arrive at the platform shortly. She had left home later than usual and had missed her bus. As Subu climbed up the steps, Chippy held her hand, as had become their routine these past few months. Chippy would wait for Subu at the station. They had first met in June, a time when rain fell with a soft beat.

The college reopened on a Tuesday, and the train was packed. Chippy held on to Subu's hand as she was caught between the moving bodies. For Subu, holding Chippy's hand felt like sinking into a comfortable sofa after walking for hours. Though she had held hands with others before, this was the first time she had felt so much at ease. She thought to herself, 'My pearl in the oyster.' And though Subaida was normally quite chatty, she didn't know Chippy's real name or what she did. Subaida had never asked her, to be honest. She had simply started calling her Chippy in one of their conversations. Holding Subaida's hands tightly was Chippy's way of answering.

Subu wondered whether Chippy couldn't speak, but then the thought would creep in that Chippy spoke to her better than anyone she knew.

Subu ran up the stairs and got into the last compartment, which smelt of iron and sunlight. The compartment at times was moved to the middle of the train when someone remembered how Saumya was raped and killed by Govindachamy on a train. It was filled with the usual people. Students were on one side and employees on the other, an unwritten code that was followed by everyone. There would be some new and unfamiliar faces every day. Although the journey began at one station and ended at another, neither station was important; it was the journey that mattered.

Those who had begun early in the morning had already opened their tiffin boxes to eat their breakfast. A few slept, turning their boredom into pillows. When she regained her breath, Subu wondered why the train hadn't started to move. Those inside began to get impatient as the train refused to spit fire and smoke. One could almost see balloons pop up above several heads with their thoughts: getting late for office; losing attendance; wondering whether to get off and take the bus to be in time for the exam.

The teacher Radhamani began the discussion for the day. 'This country will never change. Instead of providing basic amenities, they are interested in getting rich.'

'Did you hear about the note-counting machine in the minister's house?'

Vismaya began to think that no matter how many times she counted not even a single ten-rupee note doubled. She grew anxious as her already emaciated salary would grow thinner if she walked into the shop late.

'Who doesn't know this?' said Pramila, who worked in the Health Department. 'How do you think they can inaugurate their 100th or 200th jewellery store? How can they buy airplanes and helicopters? They open and close bars at will. But we pretend not to see any of this, we simply pay our taxes, and get into trains that don't move.'

'What is the fun if the train runs on time every day? Who doesn't like a change?' Jalpa winked. (You guessed it right, Jalaja and Pankaj had named their firstborn with the first syllables of their names, as if they had created something unique!)

'This is your youth talking. Don't worry. You will be tamed in a few years,' Pramila retorted.

The child sitting on the lap of a woman wearing a glittery sari began to cry. She tried to calm the baby by cooing and singing, and in between said to no one in particular, 'He is in the next compartment. It was crowded so he asked me to sit here. We are going to get a passport so that I can go to the Gulf with him.' She spoke in the dialect of Muslims from Calicut.

'Listen to her,' Mithra whispered to Theertha.

'Let her be. Not everyone is convent-educated like you.'

'Look at the child, Theertha. There are pearls and stones stitched on her frock. She has socks on her feet and a cap. She is crying because she is feeling hot. Why can't she make the child wear a cotton dress?'

'Her child, her money. We Malayalis are all the same. Haven't you been on a night train? Men wear pants with tucked-in shirts, and at times even shoes and socks. Women wear silk saris or tight jeans. Isn't it delightful to see a man wearing dhoti and kurta?'

'Yes, like the new English teacher!' Mithra pinched Theertha's thighs.

Caught off guard, Theertha let out a scream.

'What is happening?' someone asked.

'She's molesting me.'

Theertha's words echoed an oft-repeated phrase that had lost its meaning by now and instead brought laughter among the women. The child's wail rose over the laughter. Someone handed her a biscuit. The train began to move. The sigh of relief from the last compartment pushed the train forward. Someone voiced the hope the train would make up for lost time.

Whenever she became part of this confusion, Chippy would tell herself she must read *The Ladies' Coupé*. But the very next moment, she would ask herself why, especially since she was experiencing this life first-hand. She took out a book as was her wont. Amazon had delivered her a new maiden. She opened the blue cover of *The Doors of Perception* and ran her fingers over its pages; within no time, she had dived deep into it, and felt the urge to take mescaline and sit on top of the train.

As the breeze touched the sweat on their bodies, the travellers fell silent. The tired baby fell asleep. Someone's phone hummed a song. Hearing that, Vismaya asked Subu to sing a *mappila pattu*.

'Not *mappila pattu*. Sing a ghazal. That's her forte,' Jalpa intervened.

'Maybe I should go around singing "Pardesi Pardesi" in all the compartments. I can make enough money to buy my season ticket.'

Jalpa started singing as beggars did on the trains.

Susan, who worked in LIC, mocked them, 'You belong to the new generation yet your sense of humour is so old-fashioned.'

Jalpa stopped singing. 'Just like you sell policies using the same old tricks,' she retorted.

'When you get a job, you will come to me asking for a policy to cut down on your taxes.'

'I won't work. I'm trying to catch a millionaire. Then I will travel in a Mercedes Benz.'

'Be careful that you aren't trapped trying to trap him.'

'That was in the old days, when violated women were only known by the name of the place they came from. Nowadays, they are given mega offers – prime-time TV, short films, movies...'

'Children today have no ethics or values,' said Radhamani, who had retired as a teacher and was now the principal of a private school. Her ethics were as stiff as her starched khadi saris.

One of the girls whispered, 'Here comes the story of the woman who gave her bangles to Gandhiji.'

Someone showed around a WhatsApp message. 'Look, our PM has stitched his name all over his suit because he is afraid the laundry might misplace it.'

'Forward it,' was the chorus.

'Pramila! These days, creativity is confined to WhatsApp messages and Facebook posts. But don't they just last a day?'

'You are right, Zuhara. I often wonder what people will do in a couple of years when they are fed up of all this.'

'You should give us a loan to start an enterprise, Zuhara ma'am. Women empowerment, right guys?' said Mithra.

'Your daughter is doing her plus-two, right? Is she taking coaching classes?'

'No, Pramila, she is not interested in medicine. She says that education never ends and one has to think about marriage as well. If she waits till she completes her PG, she won't get a good guy. What is the use of studying engineering either? They just write bank tests. Last year, more than half the people who were recruited in my bank were engineers. I told her to study physics as there are several options thereafter.'

'Isn't that risky, Zuhara? I think a professional degree is safer. You will have to pay lakhs to get a job in a college. How can people like us afford that?' asked Susan.

'You have to see how many people pass engineering and how many get jobs.'

'Don't worry about that, Zuhara. They will increase internal marks and probably cancel the entrance test as well. They may even bring home the certificate itself.' Comrade Vrinda Rajasekharan was enraged.

'As if this place was overflowing with honey and milk when your party was ruling! I've heard of paid seats in professional colleges but now that's the case in elections as well.' Arunima was ready for battle.

'No politics, please. We are ordinary people, so sing us a song and save us,' Jalpa shook Subaida's hand, who began singing:

Woh kagaz ki kashti
Woh barish ka paani

The song filled its listeners with a desire to see the rain. The train had stopped at a station, and everyone noticed the girl waiting at the platform, who looked as if she had come straight from her wedding. She was bathed in gold; the henna on her hands was still a dark red. The sindoor on her forehead glowed as if it were the Equator line that would decide her life.

'She seems to have believed the advertisement of that jewellery shop that has discounts for customers – you know the ad in which Manju Warrier acts?' Vrinda ridiculed her.

Theertha couldn't understand why the channels had given an award to Manju. Manju had first decided not to act after getting married and then she had come back to the movies. There were so many actresses who had come back to cinema, so why had she been regarded as special?

'She is a strong woman. She came back without taking a single rupee as alimony,' said Vismaya.

Zuhara interrupted her. 'She could have brought her daughter along with her.'

Pramila agreed. 'How can a girl stay without her mother?'

'Why can't a father bring up his daughter?' Priyada sounded angry. 'Manju didn't bring her daughter as dowry when she got married. Both of them are equally responsible for her. I was in the sixth standard when my mother died. Everyone forced my father to remarry, but he never did so, saying, "I can bring up my daughter by myself." Well, I did not have any problems growing up, and I can't see anyone else in my mother's place. But when I get a job and become independent, I will definitely look for a partner for my father.'

Everyone stayed silent for a while. Vismaya felt a heaviness in her heart. She had enthusiastically started working as a salesgirl. When she wore the sari that was her uniform and stood in the air-conditioned shop between a pile of clothes, every day was a celebration for her. Every time a bride came to select a wedding sari, she got excited. When she displayed the sari on herself, she would blush as if it were her own wedding day. She felt her blouse getting tighter and grew afraid it would burst open. But when she realized she was only acting a part that was but a dream which would never become reality, she moved to the undergarments section. How could she dare to have more expensive dreams when even a bathroom break was a dream that could not be fulfilled? She hesitated to drink a drop of water even when her throat became dry, fearing she'd have to go to the bathroom. After all, how many workplaces had a clean bathroom, or even a bathroom to begin with? We have to put our bums on seats that men would have pissed all over, and the toilets would smell nauseating. She did not even have the time to realize she was growing old, and so were her dreams. Today, in the train, she felt like being a mother to this child, and felt her breasts filling with milk.

'Oh, has the train stopped again?'

'Well today is gone then.'

The tea seller passed that way.

'Why isn't the train moving?'

'There is a crossing ahead. The Chennai Mail is coming, so it will take time.'

'Should we get down and push?'

The compartment turned into an adda for the women with their laughter, jokes, whispers and sighs. Vismaya wanted to avoid the reprimands and the shouting she would get to hear at the shop and instead go to the beach. But the wretchedness of a family that depended on her stopped her.

The North Indian woman who sat in the corridor near the toilet got down to buy biscuits for her child. They sat on the floor itself and ate the biscuits after dipping them in tea. They weren't bothered by the train running late. They looked like a painting in sepia tones, the shabbily dressed mother and her child with matted hair against the corridor.

The heat of the sun was getting worse, like their impatience. A few girls got down and started walking up and down the platform. They didn't forget to look at the boys on the other side.

'Look at the third guy. He's hot.'

'Don't stare and embarrass him,' someone warned her.

The old lady who had been sleeping on the upper berth woke up, put on her glasses, and asked the people on the lower berth which station they were at. Then she started singing a prayer. She told them she had given up her profession as a doctor to spread the word of God. Vrinda pitied her, but Vismaya wanted to listen to her stories. It is not that she liked Shiva less, but she had always found Christ's compassionate face quite appealing.

When she saw Vismaya noting down the woman's number, Niranjali teased her, 'Be careful. This is the time for Ghar Vapasi.'

The conversation moved to *PK* and *Charlie Hebdo* and touched upon Subaida's head scarf. Subaida in turn said, 'This is my choice. No one finds it wrong when women wear bikinis on the beaches of Paris. So why should they find fault with me?'

Anima said, 'You can wear a purdah in Saudi but you can't wear a bikini there.'

'This veil gives me confidence. You waste so much time in front of the mirror doing your hair every morning.'

'Well, if no one looked in the mirror, those who make mirrors would starve. We have nothing but time to waste.' Jalpa steamed like potassium dropped in water. She couldn't remain still. 'Let me tell you, this purdah is of no use. I have a friend, an author, who said his greatest desire was to have sex with a woman who wears purdah.'

'There she goes boasting again. Someone please stuff some halwa down her throat,' Subaida laughed and Jalpa planted a kiss on her cheek.

'Oh, I am feeling hungry now. I want halwa, black halwa. Doesn't anybody have any snacks with them? Zuhara, your fried beef appam or mussel fry? Something? Why can't you bring stuffed bananas at least? Susan chechi, isn't your husband coming down from the Gulf any time soon? We usually get your roasted coconut and rice powder and Kuzhalappam then. You'd once brought a snack made of mango seed – I forget its name but it was superb.'

'Oh, my grandmother had brought mangoes from Kuttanad. But who has the time nowadays to pick mangoes, take out its seeds and crush them to make the appam?'

'No one is enthusiastic about such things these days.' Niranjali listed down her favourites one by one when they noticed Mithra sitting hunched up.

'What happened?'

Mithra did not reply, but clutched her stomach harder.

'If you have a stomach ache, why can't you say so? Who has a Meftal-Spas?' Niranjali asked around, and started digging into her bag. As Meftal was used by all of them, they found a tablet quickly. Someone asked Mithra if she wanted a pad. She shook her head. Some of the passengers moved to the upper berth and asked Mithra to lie down. Resting her head on Theertha's lap, Mithra cursed the vessel inside her.

Everyone began to talk about their own pains and discomforts.

Jalpa said, 'If only we could take out our uterus at will and put it back inside when needed.'

'Then women wouldn't need to fear anything. Look at how they behave even now. I was shocked when I read about the iPill. Girls go astray because of lack of faith. Deep faith…' Doctor Faith, as someone had named the doctor-turned-sanyasin, started to expound.

Niranjali jumped in. 'Isn't it because one doesn't go astray that girls become pregnant? I mean if the sperm lost its way, how would you become pregnant?'

Vrinda joined forces, 'The doctor hasn't read the chapter "A Virgin's Pregnancy".' Doctor Faith fell silent.

'I hid my periods,' said Jalpa.

'Well, does everyone wear their panties outside like Superman, Jalpa?' Niranjali teased her.

'That is not what I meant. I didn't tell anyone at home when I began menstruating.'

'What?' Everyone was shocked by her declaration. Jalpa began to narrate:

'My cousin and I are almost the same age. She was not allowed to go anywhere by herself after she got her periods. When I asked my mother, she said girls had to be careful and listed out a hundred taboos. When I reached the eighth grade, my mother would scare me every day by saying she had dreamt that I had come of age. Every time I went to the bathroom, she would wait outside anxiously. I began to believe menstruation was a monster which would take away my freedom. So when I started my periods, I didn't tell them for a long time.'

'Oh God! How did you manage? Surely you must be joking.'

'No, Susan chechi. I would buy pads and hide them. I managed for nearly six to seven months until my cousin found out.'

'Your mother? What did she say?'

'I told her that the health mission people had visited our school and distributed pads and showed us how to use them. And as I didn't need them, I told her, I put them away in the cupboard. The next time I got my periods I told her. But maybe Amma knew by then. She didn't create a fuss, just bathed me with turmeric after the period stopped.'

'I was the first amongst my cousins to get my periods, when I was in the sixth grade,' Theertha remembered. 'When I saw a red flower blooming in my panties, I told my mother. She pinched me, because I had matured before the others. I burst into tears thinking I would die. It was chechi who taught me how to use a pad. My father held me close, kissed me on my forehead and said, "You are a woman now." It was only then that I stopped crying.'

'You girls are lucky. No one is embarrassed to buy pads now. When I was a girl, we had to use cloth strips. We had to wash and dry them without anyone seeing them. We had to hide them. As a girl I would wear long slips, and at times would tie a long ribbon around my chest to cover my breasts. I had to hide my feminine growth as I lived in a house that got girls married when they matured. But I had decided to study and get a job. My daughter thankfully doesn't need to do all this,' Zuhara had mixed expressions on her face as she remembered her suppressed teenage years and the happiness at having achieved her goal.

'You are right. Life was so difficult back then. I was in sixth or seventh grade when I first heard the word *theendari*. That was what we called menstruation back then. It was a taboo to touch a menstruating woman.' Pramila stifled her laughter. 'Once, when I reached my class, there was a huge commotion. It was a convent school for girls and so there were no inhibitions. Someone said Vasanthi had menstruated. I was a slip of a girl in a half-skirt. Don't laugh. I have become fat now after two kids and all that goes with it. When I have to walk a tightrope by managing my house, work and two children, how do I find the time to take care of my figure? Anyway, I am not planning to compete for the Miss India title.'

'And Vasanthi?'

Her audience remained hooked to her tale.

'The bigger girls sat on the last two benches. The teachers scolded them almost every day. They had failed two or three years. Times were different then. You couldn't pass by adjusting the internal marks and no one would give you marks if you jotted down the question number in your answer paper. These backbencher girls wore skirts that reached their ankles. One of them, Safiya, got married and stopped coming to school.

'No one sat next to Vasanthi that day. They said she

was menstruating and no one must touch her, else we would also become unclean. Then it became a game for us. Someone would touch Vasanthi and then run to touch us. We would run away. We would wash our hands and become clean. Then we would go and touch Vasanthi again.

'Vasanthi was an untouchable for a week. We celebrated that week like a festival. We were too young to think about her feelings. Vasanthi was forbidden from even drawing water from the well. But when I got home, there was an anticlimax. I told my mother eagerly, and Amma told me it would happen to all of us every month after girls matured. The cloth used during the period has to be washed thoroughly. Snakes like the smell of blood and they would seek out the blood-stained cloth. The snake would then wind itself around the menstruating girl and would never leave her. Amma told me of several such incidents. I believed her for a long time, and lived in fear of the snake that would come looking for me. I couldn't go to the toilet or have a bath without imagining a snake lying in wait for me. Snakes slithered in my dreams. Even today I am afraid of snakes. I can't even bear to look at their pictures! But you children grew up watching advertisements of sanitary pads on TV. How would you understand all of this?'

'If you go by those ads, you would think that you can do athletics wearing those pads. But what about the pain you feel, the cramps, the PMS, and then the discomfort while travelling when you are menstruating? You can't even change your pads sometimes.'

'You are right, Susan, and you can't throw away the pads in office either as men are there. I bring them home by covering them in two to three wrappers and burn them. I wonder what women who live in flats do. The Kudumbashree workers must be taking care of the waste disposal, right? My periods are crazy, never on time. They start every time we plan a trip. Then my husband gets so irritated with me.'

'Mr Majeed must be having his own desires too,' Jalpa teased Zuhara.

As everyone laughed, Zuhara said, 'Don't change my husband's name.'

Zuhara changed the subject as she remembered a Majid she had once been in love with. She wished Basheer's famous story hadn't been turned into a movie. Now Majeed looked like the actor Mammootty whenever she thought of him.*

Vismaya wasn't thinking about superstars Mammootty or Mohanlal, but about her fast-approaching periods, which were very regular. On the first two days, it flowed like water from a broken pipe. She had to buy pads, though she could ill-afford it. She would put one pad over

---

* The film *Balyakalasakhi*, based on writer Vaikom Muhammad Basheer's story of the same name, is a love story of characters Majeed and Zuhara. Majeed is played in the movie by actor Mammootty.

the other, but one day, she felt the blood flowing down her legs. Aparna saved her from the manager's anger. Vismaya wept with embarrassment.

Noticing Vismaya's downcast expression, Priyada asked, 'What happened?'

Vismaya sighed, 'We are not permitted to use the bathroom at work.'

'We live in a country where our underwear is inspected. When women sent their pads in protest, they were mocked.'

'Anima, will men change if we send them a couple of pads? Then the celebration on Facebook by posting blood-stained napkins. I was nauseated.'

'Susan chechi, you are educated, yet you don't realize the discrimination that is practised here.'

'Aren't we also responsible? Do we speak to men at home about this? Do they see us bleeding? Our mothers asked us to hide our periods, and we repeat the same advice to our daughters. We stand embarrassed when a drop of blood stains our backside. Men have no qualms about peeing on the road.'

'True. I was lying in bed with excruciating stomach pain. My son brought me a tablet. When I asked him how he knew, he said, "I learnt in Biology."'

'That is what I said, Pramila. Why should we hesitate to tell our boys? Why do we hide our pads from them?'

Priyada agreed with Susan. 'Staining our clothes is a

nightmare. I once asked a friend to check my backside, and she pranked me by saying she could see a blood stain. I nearly died of shame.'

'That is why they posted stained napkins on Facebook. Let people look at them till the taboo disappears.'

Jalpa began an embroidered tale about her own experiences. 'Once, my skirt stained in class as I attended a workshop. A male friend went and bought pads for me.'

'Lies!' someone said from the upper berth.

Mithra had dozed off. Stroking her sweaty forehead, Theertha said, 'It's difficult when there are boys in class. Once, when our math teacher was drilling sine theta into us, I felt pain drilling into my stomach, and the cramps spread, tightening their grip. I felt dizzy and the teacher told me to lie down on the last bench. What disturbed me more than the pain was the thought that everyone knew I had got my period.'

'It was the same at our ancestral home during the Ramadan fast. You couldn't fast during those days and it was difficult to eat as well. We had to eat in a dingy room near the kitchen, or everyone would know.'

'There were so many rituals, Zuhara. In our community, when a girl matured, we had to conduct so many functions. *Thirandukalayanam* was the celebration of menarche. Most old houses had outhouses for women to stay in during their periods. I used to feel these were archaic customs, but now I feel it was better that way. You could be on your own for four to five days – you could read books, listen to music. Now, however tired you are, you have to get into the kitchen and cook breakfast and lunch. You have to pack tiffin boxes for everyone. And you have to go to work. Imagine if our husbands and the children cooked for us for four to five days.'

Susan replied, 'What a dream!'

'Excuse me, how can you even think of being outside? We are very much inside. This practice of staying in the outhouse, and this ridiculous custom of – what you called *Thirandukalayanam* – is a nonsensical patriarchal custom.'

'God, here comes Tharoor!' Jalpa whispered to Niranjali. Everyone hid a smile.

Kamala still had the hangover of studying in a central university. She would speak only in English. If at all she lapsed into Malayalam, it was an anglicized Malayalam. She pronounced her name as 'Kamla'. She was against reserving a seat for women, yet she insisted on getting into the ladies' compartment, to 'study women' as she claimed. She never showed any interest in the substandard discussions the others indulged in. Instead, she would be reading. Today she had *The Vagina* with her. Niranjali noted the cover was creative. If at all Kamala condescended to say something, she would quote Donna Haraway or Félix Guattari. (Jalpa would murmur, 'We only know Kothari who writes sex advice columns in women's magazines.')

If the discussion was about movies, Kamala would talk about Laura Mulvey, gaze, scopophilia, and quote from foreign films. Then Jalpa or Niranjali would lionize actors Shakeela and Pandit just to tease her. She was planning to make a documentary and become an activist. And she posted pictures on her Facebook page showing her armpit hair. But her words were swallowed by the train that had suddenly decided to move. Mithra got up slowly. She hadn't eaten all morning. Feeling nauseous, she struggled her way to the bathroom. Everyone else also grew nauseous thinking about the bathroom in the train.

The North Indian woman said, 'In my village, we used mud.' She had learnt enough Malayalam to understand what the others were talking about. When she heard them, she could suddenly smell her village. 'Women who couldn't afford cloth would use mud and old sacks. Water was scarce, and here, you women complain even though water flowed from pipes all the time and you could bathe or change pads whenever you wanted to.'

Everyone remained quiet thinking about their own journeys. Anima then hesitatingly voiced a question that lingered on everyone's minds: 'How do you manage, Subaida? We find it so difficult.'

Subaida blinked her sightless eyes. Turning her head to one side, she said, 'I was in a special hostel from grade one onwards. I learnt to do everything else by myself – to bathe, wash my clothes, to clean up after eating. I then joined a high school near my house. My mother explained everything to me. One day, I felt something sticky. My mother washed me and helped me put a cloth. Then I started using pads. We learn to be independent from the age of five or six.' Chippy held Subaida's hands with love.

Mithra returned, looking like a wilted flower. She rested her head on the window. 'Damn this menstruation!'

Radhamani opened her flask and gave her a cup of black coffee. She never ate anything bought on the train. 'You will realize the value of this blood only after it dries up. The red energizes us, makes us women. Even though we did not have the conveniences that you do, we never found it unendurable. After bathing on the fifth day using herbs and green leaves, we would be filled with energy. Each cell of our body would be filled with the exhilaration of being a woman. I don't know why, whether it was because we did hard labour or gave birth to five or six children, we never felt any difficulty. As you tease me, I couldn't give my bangles to Gandhiji only because I was born too late. But I have participated in many protests. I married my colleague who was the same age as me. When all this stopped, I felt a burning sensation come over me, as if my body was on fire. The monthly bloodletting kept my body supple. But men are always young; he gets irritated and sleeps on the other side of the bed facing the wall. I go to work not because I need money, but to remind myself that I have a life beyond my body.'

The train reached its destination. Niranjali kissed Radhamani's wrinkled cheek.

'It's 11 a.m. Why should we go to college or work? Let us go for a movie, eat lunch, go to the beach and go home in the evening.'

They thought about their work schedule and the hundred things they had to do that day. Then they thought, 'Why can't we spend a day for ourselves?'

Vrinda peeled off the red bindi from her forehead and stuck it on the wall of the women's compartment. She announced, 'Let the menstrual train depart. Today is our day.' All of them cheered, roaring with laughter.

The men looked at them questioningly, but the women were impervious to their glances.

ACKNOWLEDGEMENTS

I wish to extend my gratitude and love to –

Inha, who would have loved to see the book. Wish she were around for a few more years.

Divya, for introducing me to Priya.

Priya, my translator, whom I met only after the work was done, during one of the lit fests. We had a whole day to chat and ended up planning a trip to Istanbul!

Anees Salim, for the wonderful foreword and the support he extended.

Kanishka Gupta, for his initiative in making this book possible.

Amish Mulmi, for his insightful suggestions.

Sonali Jindal, my editor, and Sini Nair at Hachette.

Bunch of friends.

The Djinn, who comes and goes at his whim, making me inspired or dejected.

The three men in my life, Aman, Aamir and Rafiq, who let me be (do they have another choice!).